GATOR BAIT ...

Just as Clint was about to pull the trigger, he felt a shooting pain at the back of his ankles and suddenly the world was turned onto its ear.

His body toppled backward over a log that had been hidden beneath a carpet of moss to blend in perfectly with the rest of the shadows. When his back hit the ground, all the air was knocked out of his lungs. He couldn't feel anything but sharp pains lancing through most of his body. All he could hear was the quick, solid footsteps of the hungry gator scampering toward him.

Clint tried to sit up and fire the shotgun, but the weight of the animal was already pressing down on top of him, pinning him down beneath a solid mass of muscles and scaly flesh. . . .

DON'T MISS THESE
ALL-ACTION WESTERN SERIES
FROM THE BERKLEY PUBLISHING GROUP

THE GUNSMITH by J. R. Roberts
Clint Adams was a legend among lawmen, outlaws, and ladies.
They called him . . . the Gunsmith.

LONGARM by Tabor Evans
The popular long-running series about U.S. Deputy Marshal
Long—his life, his loves, his fight for justice.

SLOCUM by Jake Logan
Today's longest-running action Western. John Slocum rides
a deadly trail of hot blood and cold steel.

BUSHWHACKERS by B. J. Lanagan
An action-packed series by the creators of Longarm! The
rousing adventures of the most brutal gang of cutthroats ever
assembled—Quantrill's Raiders.

DIAMONDBACK by Guy Brewer
Dex Yancey is Diamondback, a southern gentleman turned
con man when his brother cheats him out of the family fortune. Ladies love him. Gamblers hate him. But nobody pulls
one over on Dex . . .

WILDGUN by Jack Hanson
Will Barlow's continuing search for his daughter, kidnapped
by the Blackfeet Indians who slaughtered the rest of his family.

THE GUNSMITH

235

BAYOU GHOSTS

J. R. ROBERTS

JOVE BOOKS, NEW YORK

BAYOU GHOSTS

A Jove Book / published by arrangement with
the author

PRINTING HISTORY
Jove edition / July 2001

All rights reserved.
Copyright © 2001 by Robert J. Randisi.
This book, or parts thereof, may not be reproduced in any form
without permission.
For information address: The Berkley Publishing Group,
a division of Penguin Putnam Inc.,
375 Hudson Street, New York, New York 10014.

The Penguin Putnam Inc. World Wide Web site address is
www.penguinputnam.com

ISBN: 0-515-13104-0

A JOVE BOOK®
Jove Books are published by The Berkley Publishing Group,
a division of Penguin Putnam Inc.,
375 Hudson Street, New York, New York 10014.
JOVE and the "J" design
are trademarks belonging to Penguin Putnam Inc.

PRINTED IN THE UNITED STATES OF AMERICA

10 9 8 7 6 5 4 3 2 1

ONE

The last time Clint Adams had seen Joseph Terray was a little more than three years ago. There had been some trouble on a cattle drive from West Texas up to Kansas and by the time Joseph had made it to Dodge City, he was shot, beaten and completely penniless. That was the condition he was in when Clint first met him. The sheriff had pleaded with Clint to head up a posse and go after the rustlers who'd been responsible for stealing well over ten thousand head of cattle, not counting the herd Joseph had been driving. Before Clint headed out, Joseph insisted on coming along to personally get his hands on the men who'd robbed him.

The rustlers' trail led them all the way back to Texas and ended without so much as a fight. Mostly, that was due to the fact that the leader of the rustlers recognized Clint on sight and decided to take his chances with a judge rather than draw down on the Gunsmith.

Joseph's home was a day's ride over the Texas border in a little town called Byers, Louisiana. It was in the middle of the bayou and the spirited Cajun insisted that Clint follow him there to let him pay him back properly for saving his livelihood. Since he didn't have any money, all he could offer was hospitality. Clint was more concerned with the possibility of stray rustlers catching up to Joseph when he was riding alone, so he followed him home to take him up on his offer. When he got the first bite of Joseph's wife's cooking in his mouth,

Clint swore that it was the best detour he'd ever taken.

Joseph told him to look him up the next time he was in the area and, well, here he was. Clint had been riding through the northern part of Louisiana on his way back to Labyrinth, Texas, and got to thinking about what he could do to pass a few hours before heading home when the name Joseph Terray came to mind. He could still taste those black-eyed peas and corn bread. The thick, spicy shrimp gumbo and lime pie still hadn't been matched by any other cook Clint had found in the time that had passed, and thinking about those smells and tastes had caused his mind to drift away as if trying to hide from the sticky film of salty sweat covering his body from head to toe.

Eclipse seemed to be enjoying the leisurely pace that Clint had allowed him to take as they rode through the lush, green landscape along the Mississippi River. The land had turned into swamp a few miles ago and both horse and rider seemed to have been infected by the easy-going mind-set that came along with the oppressive humidity in the air. The air felt thicker than the cloudy, catfish-infested waters of the river and trying to move too fast did as much good as trying to swim quickly through molasses, so why bother.

It was the end of August and the summer was drawing to a close. Further up north, the nights had begun to take on a welcome chill. But this far down below the Mason Dixon, relief from the sticky heat was still a long ways off, which prompted most folks in the area to keep moving from shady spot to shady spot just so they weren't boiled in their own juices. At least that seemed to be the sentiment of most everyone that Clint passed since he'd entered Louisiana.

His first thought had been to keep riding and let Eclipse get his exercise while shaving a few days off the length of his trip. But as the day wore on, the blue sky overhead seemed to press down on both their backs, burning the back of Clint's neck and arms with its balmy touch. The flies got big enough to cut the air as they passed and the sweet smell of the lush vegetation along the trail made his eyelids hang lower with every passing hour.

By the time the afternoon had gone, all thought of a quick run through the state had been burned from Clint's mind. Eclipse's tail swished lazily from side to side in a losing battle to keep the hungry mosquitoes off his flank while the stallion's hooves clomped into the rich Louisiana clay.

If his memory served him correctly, Clint knew the little town of Byers sat right on the edge of the bayou about a day's ride south of where he was. He could head there to catch up on old times with Joseph over a home-cooked dinner or spend another four nights sleeping on the ground while heading straight into Labyrinth. Although he didn't really mind spending some time under the stars, Clint could smell Kim Terray's legendary gumbo as if he still had some of the smoke from her cooking fires clinging to his shirt.

Suddenly—his stomach growling—the decision did not seem such a hard one to make.

"Okay, boy," Clint said to the Darley Arabian he'd gotten as a gift from the infamous P. T. Barnum, "we're making a little detour."

TWO

Even though the sun had set long ago, the air in the small two-room cabin was as warm and sticky as it would have been anywhere else at high noon. But the cabin wasn't just anywhere else. It was on the outskirts of Byers, Louisiana, which also meant it was sharing the same swamp and marshland with all the gators that infested the tangled bush of the bayou.

Joseph Terray had lived his entire life in those swamps. In the same town. Even in the same cabin, which had been given to him by his parents as a wedding present before the old folks had moved on to live with Joseph's brother in New Orleans. The little cabin was made of timber, covered in a hard shell of mold and other mosses which covered just about everything else in the bayou that made the mistake of standing still too long.

Everything there was alive, from the breezes laden with mosquitoes and fireflies to the soil which crawled with more forms of slugs and salamanders than most folks knew existed. The still, murky waters held on to the moonlight without so much as a ripple to distort its reflection. A fallen tree lay along the banks, its top edge chipped away and worn down into a long bench where Joseph and his wife could sit and smell the sweet, tangy scent of the bayou.

Nobody was on the bench at the moment, though.

It was well past midnight. Joseph Terray and his wife Kimberly were inside the cabin, their lantern turned down to give the windows a dim flickering glow. While the cicadas droned on in their monotonous rhythm, the Terray's were lying beside the dying embers of their fire, making their own rhythm to add to the night's.

Kim was laying facedown on top of a large blanket that had been spread out over the floor in front of the hearth. Behind her, the kitchen table had been pushed against one of the walls, giving Joseph plenty of space to move as he crawled around her body, moving his hands over Kim's richly tanned skin.

She wore a simple cotton slip that clung to her figure, held close to her skin by a thin film of sweat. As Joseph peeled the material down off her shoulders, he ran his tongue down the back of her neck. Kim had a naturally sweet flavor which now mingled with a sharp saltiness. When her husband ran his hands along her sides to pull the top of her slip down even further, Kim made a noise in the back of her throat that was one part moan and another part growl.

Joseph slid her clothing down until it was bunched up at her waist and took in the sight of her body. Flickering firelight played off Kim's sloping breast as she raised upon her elbows, and she moaned a little louder when Joseph's hands found them. He'd already tossed his shirt across the small room and could feel his own perspiration running over his barrel chest.

Getting to his feet, he walked around so that he could see his wife's face as he undressed in front of her. Joseph had the physique of any man who'd had to forge a life in a land as harsh as the bayou. Although he only stood a few inches taller than his wife, his broad shoulders gave him a hulking appearance that Kim had always found exciting. He cut his own hair every week with a straight-edge razor and it showed. In fact, the thick tangle on his face which passed for a beard was considerably longer than the matted mess on top of his head. Sinewy forearms, covered with scars and gator bites, flexed in the dim light.

Unable to wait any longer, Kim got up to her knees and reached out to loosen Joseph's belt. Her dark red hair flowed carelessly over her shoulders and large, pendulous breasts swung as she worked his buckle open. She was beyond words as she pulled his clothing to the floor, grunting in satisfaction at the sight of his hard shaft in front of her face.

After licking her lips with a loud smack, Kim leaned forward and took his swollen head into her mouth. She teased his cock with her tongue, swirling it around and down its length before moving her lips all the way to the base of his shaft. Joseph leaned his head back and dug his fingers through her hair. When he felt her throat constrict around him, he held her by the back of the head until she started pulling away.

"Come down here with me," she said as her hands reached up to grab him by the waist and guide him to the blanket next to her.

Once he was laying on his back, Kim moved on top of him, straddling his muscular chest. She rubbed herself against him, a carnal smile playing across her lips, as she inched her body forward until his beard was tickling her thighs. With one hand, she reached back to massage his stomach and with the other, she grabbed the top of Joseph's head and pulled his face between her legs.

He opened his mouth eagerly and felt her hot, wet pussy grinding against his lips. When he stuck his tongue inside of her, Kim arched her back and let out a groan that rivaled that of any of the bayou's wildlife. She kept right on moaning until her voice raised into a scream and her hips were bucking wildly onto Joseph's mouth.

Giving her hips a playful slap, he pushed her off of him and got to his feet just long enough for Kim to crawl beneath him. She took her position on her back with her legs spread wide, opening herself to accept his solid thickness. He dropped down and grabbed hold of her breasts while moving his hips until he could feel his pole pushing gently into her. Joseph leaned forward, kissed his wife hard on the mouth and thrust his hips forward to bury himself deeply between her legs.

Now they were both crying out, their voices overpowering all the other noises in the swamp as their flesh pounded together. Kim was the loudest and she raked her nails across his back while giving in completely to the pleasures that ravaged her body and the cries that reddened her throat.

Joseph dug his fingers into the blanket on either side of her her head as he drove deeper and deeper into her, straining to bury himself further into her warmth. He raised his upper body and saw Kim with her arms stretched out over her head, screaming at the height of her pleasure, her muscles jumping wildly beneath her skin.

Their carnal screams were loud enough to make the cicadas stop their song for a moment. They were loud enough to fill the cabin with the rhythm of their rough dance and they were loud enough to drown out the sound of their door being pushed open to let three men walk inside.

Kim's legs were still wrapped tightly around Joseph's back as he was pulled to his feet by rough hands grabbing him under both arms. Only when she felt the weight of her husband's body being lifted off of her did she open her eyes to see the strangers assaulting her lover. She kept screaming, except her tone changed from passion to terror.

Both men that she could see were well over six feet tall. They dressed in dirty brown and black clothing, with shirts buttoned all the way to their necks as if in an effort to look better for company. One of the men had a gambler's string tie around his neck and the other sported a knee-length coat that was encrusted with dark patches of mud.

Kim's screams got even louder when she saw the men's faces. Neither one of them looked as though they'd seen a decent meal for years. Pale, chalky skin was stretched tight over their skulls. Eyes peered out from deep inside their sockets without the slightest hint of emotion. They strangers looked more than sick or malnourished. They looked dead.

Now, Kim's screams rattled the glass of both the cabin's windows.

THREE

Naked and hanging suspended between the two men, Joseph Terray kicked his feet wildly while twisting in their grasp. All he could see from his position was the bony hands under his arms and his wife crying in terror, her body drawn up into a defensive ball.

"Let me go, you sons a bitches!" he yelled while thrashing from side to side.

Just as he was about to break free of the hands, Joseph was dropped to the floor. He was barely able to keep his legs beneath him as he spun around with a wild snarl and clenched his fists. The sight of the two pale strangers was enough to make him pause before throwing himself toward them. When they stepped to either side, he could see a third man standing behind them, pointing a gun at Joseph's chest.

"Calm yerself before I put you down," the third man said.

Joseph's instincts screamed at him to get the strangers out of his home no matter who they were or what they wanted. Then his common sense reminded him of the gun being pointed his way. Without taking his eyes off the men, Joseph stepped back until he could touch Kim's side with the back of his heel.

She'd already pulled her slip over her body, but was unable to keep the tears from flowing down her face. "Who are they, Joe?" she asked hysterically as though she didn't think the men could hear. "What do they want from us?"

The man holding the gun stood slightly taller than Joseph, but a bit shorter than the men on either side of him. He wore a long, black undertaker's coat and a dirty priest's collar around his neck. Scrawled on the grimy white collar were dark red markings made in what looked like clotted blood. His face had even less color than his men's and his filthy hair came down in greasy braids past his shoulders. Under his coat, the man wore a black vest and gray shirt, both of which were punctured by old bullet holes.

When the man smiled, his face resembled a gator's. His sharp, crooked teeth looked like they belonged inside a lizard's mouth instead of a man's. "Ah'll answer that question, ma'am," he said with a thick Cajun accent. "M'name's Mason Rhyse. Maybe you heard'a me?"

All of the rage had drained from Joseph's face, right along with the color in his cheeks. "I heard of you. Everyone has."

Behind Joseph, Kim looked on with eyes that had become round as saucers. "Oh my God," she whispered while crossing herself.

Joseph took a long look at the men who had picked him up and dropped him onto the ground. He recognized them. But, those couldn't possibly be the men he was thinking of.

Nodding, Rhyse smiled his gator smile and glared at Joseph with a cruel glint in his eyes. "You seen dem faces before, eh? Perhaps you knew dem before I get my hands on 'em?"

Joseph shook his head. He'd seen the other two before, all right. He'd seen one of them around the saloon in Byers and another at a trading post in the next town over. He'd never talked to them or even gotten to know much about them, but he'd heard their names plenty of times. People had talked about those men a lot, especially right after they'd been called out and shot dead by a man who'd killed a priest to get in good with the devil.

Willie Stokes had lived in Byers and had been killed in his home a few months ago. Joseph had been to the funeral. The entire town had been hungry for justice when one of their own was executed in his own house. That hunger turned into something else the night after the services when Stokes's mother went to put fresh flowers on his grave, only to find an empty wooden tomb set on top of ground that was too wet to accept a burial.

Talk of voodoo curses and zombies spread through the town, only to become hysteria when Ed Lovario was murdered by the same priest killer who'd done in poor Stokes. Just like before, the body was put into its crude wooden box and set in line with the other tombs in what the locals used as a graveyard. The next time the sun rose, it shone down on broken planks and a trail of blood leading deep into the swamp.

The stories came fast and furious, but they soon joined the other local legends as gruesome entertainments on dark nights. Everyone knew what had happened, but didn't have a clue about what to do about it. Plenty of locals said they'd seen the dead men riding their dead horses in search of offerings to take back to Satan. Word had it that if you'd give them what they wanted, the man named Rhyse would take his risen corpses and leave you in peace. If you fought them, you'd be getting into more bad voodoo than any priestess could get you out of.

Now, Joseph looked at the body of Willie Stokes as it stood in front of him, dressed in the same string tie he'd been buried in. "It's really you," he said, in awe of the horrific turn his life had taken. "Damn, Willie, what happened? How can you be here?"

Stokes, a tall black man in his late twenties, let out a breath that seemed to deflate his entire chest. Where his skin had once been dark and rich, it was now pasty and flaking off around his eyes and mouth. "You heard the stories," Stokes said in a deep, trembling voice. "They all true. Mista Rhyse brought me back sure as I'm standin' here. Now, he come for you."

Joseph managed to tear his eyes away from the three men so he could look at his wife. Terrified beyond reason, Kim had backed herself up against a wall. Upon hearing those last words coming from the dead man's lips, she got up and rushed over to her husband, wrapping her arms tightly around his body.

"We'll give you whatever you want," she screamed to Rhyse. "I heard the stories and you can take anything we have, just leave us alone!"

Stepping from behind his men, Rhyse held his gun near his hip. He smelled like the over-ripe vegetation in the bayou and when he got closer, little insects could be seen crawling through his long, matted hair. "You ain't got enough to turn me away," he said through his dirty grin. "What I want is you, Joseph Terray. Come along now and we'll leave your pretty wife alone. If not, den we'll see what kinda things a dead man can do with 'dat sweet body of hers."

Joseph forgot about all of the stories he'd been told. He couldn't think of anything else but the rage that had re-ignited in his soul at hearing Rhyse talk about his wife. "Dead man or not," Joseph snarled, "I'm gonna tear you apart if you take one more step toward her."

Rhyse glared into Joseph's eyes as if he was peering into his soul. "You see this collar aroun' my neck? You know who that belong to. You know what I done in my life. What make you think there's anything you can do to me worse than what I already seen? You think I don't hear that priest cursin' me from beyond every second my eyes are open? What you gonna do that's worse than that?

"You gonna shoot me? You gonna shoot him?" Rhyse asked while pointing over his shoulder at the tall, pale figure of Willie Stokes. "Or him?" Now, he hooked his thumb toward Ed Lovario. By the time Rhyse had finished the question, both of his men already had their guns out.

Slipping his pistol back into its holster, Rhyse put his clammy hands on Joseph's shoulders. "Do yourself a favor," he said. "Do your wife a favor. Just give me a minute of your time."

Joseph turned, but refused to take his eyes off the pale man in front of him. "Wait in the next room, baby," he said to his wife. "You see anyone come back there that ain't me, you blow them off their feet with that rifle of mine, y'hear?"

"I'm not leaving you," Kim said, her voice shaking almost as much as the rest of her. "I won't just—"

"Do it!" Joseph shouted at her more fiercely than he'd ever done before. "Just do as I tell you and get that rifle. I'll be back soon."

Something landed at his feet and when Joseph looked down to see what it was, he found his clothes wadded into a ball on the floor.

"Put them on," Rhyse said as he backed up a few steps.

Joseph got dressed after he saw Kim was huddled on their bed with a large hunting rifle gripped in both hands. As much as he wanted to go in and give her a gentle kiss, or even run his fingers through her hair, he forced himself to stay put.

"Now what do you want?" he asked as he approached the table where Rhyse and his three men were standing.

"I want you ta join me, Joseph. Me and Stokes and Ed here are making quite a name for ourselves, but we need another by our side."

Taking a breath, Joseph forced himself to speak in a steady, controlled voice. "I'm no good with guns. And I'm no thief."

"Course you ain't no thief, but we all got to change sometime before we rot away like the rest of the swamp here. An' you don't need to be good with no gun."

"Why me?"

"Why any of us?" Lovario said in a raspy croak. When the tall man spoke, his pale white skin dropped off of him in little flakes. A thick mustache crusted with dirt trembled with every angry word. "None of us can refuse the man that's cursed us! We just do as he say till he decide to let us go."

Rhyse silenced him with a wave of his hand. "Let's not get our tempers up," he said while producing a dented copper flask from inside his vest. "How 'bout a nice drink to calm your nerves?"

Joseph took the flask, knowing it was what Rhyse wanted, and took a tentative sip. The whiskey was hot on his throat and did wonders in settling his nerves. It was the last thing he tasted before gunfire blasted through his ears.

FOUR

The trail Clint had been following eventually faded away into a set of ruts that were barely visible through the lush overgrowth and wet mud. Having spent the night in a rented room in a town that was about as big as most people's backyards, he focused in on Kim Terray's cooking as a reason why any sensible man would purposely go through all this trouble.

As the day wore on, Clint felt the kinks in his back from the lumpy mattress work themselves out during his ride. In fact, compared to the bed in that boardinghouse, the saddle was a comfortable change for his sore bones and he was actually starting to get used to the smell of the thickening Louisiana swamps.

After a while, the air started smelling rich and full of life. It hummed with buzzing wings and even the heat seemed to be just another part of the landscape rather than the oppressive burden it had been the day before.

By the time he'd ridden through more than half of the day, Clint was glad he'd decided on this particular detour. It had been a while since he'd last seen this part of the country and the fact that he was checking in on an old friend made things seem all the better. He was just starting to make plans for a further excursion to New Orleans when the town of Byers appeared in the distance.

The first sight he caught of the place was a crooked old shack half-hidden in the thick trees. It had a sagging roof and holes in the walls, which exposed glimpses of movement from inside. At first, Clint thought he was hearing more chirping insects and croaking frogs, but soon the noise took on a rhythm of its own. When he got closer, he could definitely hear the sounds of a banjo and guitar playing a slow tune to accompany a scratchy-voiced singer.

The rutted path Eclipse was on hooked around the battered old building, leading around front where it widened into a street just big enough for two horses to pass each other comfortably. Byers hadn't changed much since the last time Clint had been there. It was still full of more toads than people and smelled like the bottom of a hollow, rotted stump.

The leaning shack Clint had first seen was the saloon, which sat at the head of Byers like a proud old man. The town's main street had been named Widest since that was exactly what it was. None of the other twisting paths between the buildings were even big enough to be named at all, but the town itself did have a lot more than one would expect for being stuck in the middle of the bayou.

Besides the saloon, there was a gambling den with an up-stairs brothel, two small restaurants and a medicine shop run by the local voodoo woman named Cleo. There were other storefronts, but not any others that had a sign. Clint surveyed the little stretch of moss-covered buildings and swung down from Eclipse. When his boots hit the ground, they sunk in about half an inch and made a wet, sucking sound as he walked.

The hitching post in front of the saloon was nearly as wide as the building itself. For a town the size of Byers, there was a surprisingly large amount of horses tethered to the thick pole that was attached to two solidly planted posts. Looking around, Clint soon realized that this was the only place on the entire street where horses could be tied securely. While there were a lot of horses there, the number wasn't quite so big when he figured that post was the town's equivalent of a livery.

The entrance looked more like someone's front porch than a bar, although there wasn't anyone currently sitting in the three rickety chairs lined up outside. Inside, the saloon was brightened by the beams of sun poking in from between loose planks in the walls. Taking up slightly less than half the room was a solidly built bar with a swirling design carved into the

sides and a shiny brass rail running along the bottom. Clint
stared at it for a second, swearing to himself that he'd seen a
similar one in a hotel in New York. If the bar had been anywhere else, it would have been impressive. For the town of
Byers, it was a wonder.

The musicians that Clint had heard from outside were in the
back corner of the room. Against the wall was a man playing
banjo who looked to be older than the swamp and just about
as pretty. Sitting on a small stool was a young black man
playing guitar. His eyes went immediately to Clint and stayed
there as if waiting for something. Instead of figuring out what
that something was, Clint turned to look at the woman doing
the singing.

She was a busty redhead packed into a tan cotton dress. Her
breasts swelled beneath the fabric of her clothing and her hips
swayed in time to the song. Her dark red hair was brushed
smoothly behind her ears and tied back with a strip of leather.
Judging by the weepy lyrics she was singing and the faraway
look in her eyes, Kim Terray's mind was on a whole lot more
than her performance.

There were a few other men there, one of whom was talking
to a skinny, bald man in his thirties with a grizzled blond beard
standing behind the ornate bar. When Clint stepped up to put
his foot on the brass rail, the bartender cut his conversation
short and walked to stand in front of him.

"You need directions?" the skinny man asked.

"Only if they come with a beer," Clint said.

While filling a tin mug, the bartender spoke with an easy
drawl. "Most folks that I don't recognize are lost. Mostly they
come through here to see how to get headed back toward
wherever they was goin'."

"Well I'm not lost. I'm here to see some friends of mine."

"Who'd that be?"

Clint took a sip off the top of the mug and let the warm
beer swirl in his mouth. It tasted like it had been made earlier
that day by someone with a rusty set of pipes and washbasins.
After swallowing, he turned to look at the full-figured redhead
and then back at the barkeep. "Her."

By the time it settled in his throat, the taste of the brew had
grown on Clint in a strange sort of way. It sure beat the hell

out of the swampy flavor he'd gotten in his mouth from the day's ride.

"You're here to see Kim? I guess you heard about poor Joey, huh?"

Clint froze with his mug halfway to his mouth. "Heard what?"

The bartender got a look on his face like he'd spoken out of turn. But beyond that there was something else. Something that looked a lot like fear playing at the corner of his eyes.

One of the other drinkers, a gnarled old miner with skin that looked like it had been stripped off an alligator carcass, turned to stare the bartender in the face. "We don't want no talk o' him in here!"

Footsteps approached Clint from behind and it was then that he realized the music had stopped. "Quiet down, Ben," Kim scolded as she smacked the miner on the shoulder. "He doesn't know what happened, no matter how many times you've told the story."

Clint turned to look at Kim Terray. The redhead couldn't help but look beautiful, even in the black shawl that covered most of her body. He was surprised when she stepped up and put her arms around him, holding a little too tight and for a little too long. When she pulled away, her face was wet with tears.

"What's the matter?" Clint asked. "Where's Joseph?"

"He's dead. Got shot last night and now he's gone forever."

"My god, I'm so sorry. When's the funeral?"

The old miner spoke without turning to look at them, spitting his words onto the bar. "Can't have no funeral. Not without a body."

FIVE

Since Kim was done singing, she was through with the saloon. She'd never been a drinker and had only put up with the place because it was the only place in town where she could sing without the songs having to be out of a hymnal. She didn't say much as she led Clint out to the street and was quiet all the way through town until they reached a small road heading south into the swamp.

Once there, she stopped and stared out at the wet vegetation as the sun cast its glow onto the backs of all the passing creatures trying to hide from its rays.

"Are you going to tell me about Joseph?" Clint asked.

"You'd probably think I was crazy if you heard me say it. Hell, I've been thinking I'm crazy, myself."

"This just happened last night? The way people talk about it, you'd think it was a legend or something."

"Folks 'round here don't like to deal with what they don't understand. My Joseph died only one night ago. He was killed by known men, but he ain't dead. Not the way he's supposed to be."

Clint shook his head in confusion. "What's that supposed to mean?"

When she spoke, Kim didn't look at Clint or even in his direction. It was more like she was telling her story to the bayou, just to hear herself say it out loud rather than inform anyone in particular. "My Joey was a simple man. You met him, so you know that's the truth. He never done nothin' to nobody and the only time he ever left this town was when he needed to drive cattle to earn money to live on.

"He ain't never had much excitement in his life, 'cept when he rode with you that once. He'd talk about that when he was drunk, but hardly anyone ever believed he'd ridden with the likes of Clint Adams."

Clint nodded and watched her speak. Her voice was calm and quiet, yet only slightly tinged with sadness. "So what happened to him?" Clint asked.

"He rode the cattle up north one more time after you left and we've been livin' off that money since then. It don't take much to survive here. But last night, we weren't doing anything but our own business when Mason Rhyse came in and took my Joey away from me. He didn't have no reason. He did it because he could."

"Wait a second," Clint said as he grabbed Kim by the shoulders and forced her to look at him. "You know who did this?"

"Everyone knows."

"Then why not do something about it? Everyone in this town acts like they watch their own get killed every day and don't give a damn. Is there anyone looking for this Rhyse?"

"Ain't nobody that stupid."

Frustration was beginning to rattle Clint's nerves and he had to force himself to keep from yelling at the widow. "What did that man in the saloon mean when he said there wasn't a body?"

As soon as he asked the question, Clint wished he hadn't. Kim crossed her arms over her chest as if her heart hurt so bad it was about to leap out of her. She turned her face toward the ground as the tears came gushing out.

"Kim, I'm sorry," he said while putting a hand on her shoulder. "I didn't mean to upset you, but I just want to know what happened here. It seems there's a lot more going on than murder."

Taking a deep breath, she wiped her face with the backs of her hands and moved a stray piece of hair out of her eyes. "There is a lot more going on. If my Joey was killed, I'd learn to deal with it . . . in time. But what happened to him . . . I wouldn't wish it on my worst enemy."

When she told Clint about the previous night, Kim stared

straight ahead and spoke in a slow monotone. She didn't leave out a single detail and the further she got into the story, the more descriptive she became. However, Clint soon realized that the pain must have been too fresh inside the woman, because when she described Mason Rhyse and his men, she painted pictures of men who'd ridden straight out of hell.

But still, Clint listened. Without saying a word, he rubbed Kim's back and focused his eyes on the same distant point on the horizon that she did. He soaked in every word and tried to sort out what useful information he could as she went on to tell him about the last time she'd seen her husband's face.

"Rhyse reached into his pocket," she said, voicing the killer's name as though it was a curse, "and took out a flask of whiskey. Joey didn't want to drink it, but it was what Rhyse wanted, so he took a swig. Maybe he thought the more he obeyed that devil, the better chance I had of surviving."

"Did they threaten you?"

"I was curled up on the bed with the rifle clutched to me like it was my firstborn. I could only hear bits of what they was saying, but I saw every one of those three look my way. They had death in their eyes."

"Then what happened after Joe took his drink?"

"They led him outside. Carried him off like he was already drunk. Joey tried to struggle, but them others were too big. Too strong. They hauled him off like he was a baby and took him outside." Now, Kim had to clench her eyes tightly shut and grit her teeth as the worst moment of her life replayed itself in her mind.

"There's only two windows in my cabin," she said. "I got myself off that bed and looked through the one over my cedar chest. For a moment, when I saw them drag him by, I clutched that rifle in my hands and thought I could gun them all down. Then one of them looked at me, the one that used to be Ed Lovario, and I saw his eyes." When Kim turned to look at Clint, her own eyes had glazed over.

Inside her, Clint saw mortal fear and a fanatical tranquility. It was the look of someone who'd been afraid of the dark her entire life only to find out one day that she'd been right to do so.

"He didn't have no soul," she said in a tense whisper.

Clint kept his own eyes calm and even. He didn't want to

add any more emotions to the ones she already had. "Then what happened? Go on and tell me."

She broke eye contact and the intensity melted from her. "They took him around back, where there ain't no windows and then I heard the gunshots. There was two of 'em and each time I jumped out of my skin."

"Did they say anything when they were outside? Was there anything else you could hear before or after?"

Kim shook her head. "Just the gunshots. When they drug my Joey back, they laid him out in front of my window and I could see the blood and he wasn't moving . . ." The sobbing fits began to wrack her entire body. "They left him there and then Rhyse told the others it was time to leave. Said they'd be back for Joey after he'd had some time to rot."

As much as Clint hated to prolong the widow's pain, he needed to get the entire story. He knew this might well be the only chance that she would feel like talking about that night for a good, long time. "Kim, did you go to him? After they left, did you go to Joseph?"

She nodded. "Yes. I felt his blood and I kissed his cheek. He wasn't breathin'. His heart wasn't beatin'. But the wounds. They were . . ." Trailing off, she seemed to be drifting far away from what her life had become.

"What about the wounds, Kim?"

"They were . . . gone. And by mornin', so was the body."

SIX

Clint had seen a lot of murders in his day. He'd killed a lot of men that needed to die and had mourned those who didn't, but he hadn't seen anything quite like this.

After Kim was done with her story, she'd spent the next few minutes in Clint's arms. Neither of them spoke, which didn't matter because for the moment there wasn't a whole lot to be said. After all, how does a man respond to a tale of murder and body theft? Rather than trying to come up with an answer, Clint kept quiet and held Kim until her tears stopped falling onto his shirt.

Finally, she pulled away and started walking back toward the saloon.

"Wait," Clint said.

She stopped, but didn't turn around.

"Can I get a look at your cabin?" he asked. "Maybe see if I can find someone to help me locate the men that killed Joseph?"

Her voice was soft and full of pain. "You can go there. Lord knows I'll never step foot anywhere near it again. But as for finding Rhyse and his killers, trust me, you don't want to do that."

"I may not have known Joseph that well, but there's something very wrong about all of this."

"You're damn right there is."

"Well, it's been my experience that men like these don't do

21

things like this and go away. This Rhyse is gearing up for something bigger than walking into people's homes and murdering them in the night. At the very least, they'll kill again and if I can do something about it, I will."

She took a deep breath and gave him directions to the cabin that she'd once shared with her husband.

"Where will you be?" Clint asked once she was through.

"I'm stayin' with friends in town. Ask Emmett, he's the bartender. He knows where I'm at and I'll let him know he can tell you whatever you need. If I'm not asleep, though, I'll be in that saloon. Singin' takes my mind off things."

"I'll do my best to find Rhyse. What happened to Joseph is a crime that someone needs to pay for."

Even from where he was standing behind her, Clint could almost see the look on Kim's face. By the way she stood, the way she held her head, the slight tremble in her muscles, all of it told him she was a mess of hurt and confusion. Then she turned to look at him over her shoulder and her eyes told Clint that he'd been right.

"You only met my Joey once," she stated. "Why do more than anyone else in town's willin' to do when they've known him all his life?"

"Because from what I've seen, they're all scared. I'm not. And besides, I don't do too well just standing by to let men get away with murder, no matter who it was that got killed. It's just not my way."

"Then, thank you. Thank you from the bottom of my heart. If my Joey could say the words, I know he'd thank you too."

Although the way to the Terray's cabin seemed familiar, Clint would never have been able to find his way there without Kim's directions. In the last year, the swamp had taken over the trail he and Joseph had used last time, along with the next few trails after that by the looks of the tangled weeds and washed-out paths beneath his feet.

His first instinct had been to leave Eclipse behind, simply because the cabin wasn't that far away and Clint needed to stretch his legs after his ride into town. With only a little over a mile and a half to go, Clint thought the walk would do him some good. Then he remembered just how long a mile and a half could seem with the bayou grabbing at your boots, so he rode Eclipse as far as he could before tying the stallion to a thick, moss-covered tree.

Even though there was less than half a mile left, covering the distance on foot did not appeal to Clint.

Not at all.

At times, the overhanging trees were so think, they nearly blocked out the sun. More than once Clint nearly drew his gun on footsteps that were scrambling up behind him, only to turn and find himself staring at the cold beady eyes of a gator only slightly shorter in length than Eclipse. Luckily, the gators were distracted by something that looked like it would put up less of a fight and was more in its reach. Either that, or the big scaly monster simply wasn't hungry at the moment.

Clint nearly walked right past the old cabin, even though he wasn't more than fifteen feet away from it. Kim had told him to look for the flattened out log along the side of the marsh. If not for that landmark, Clint would have walked by the cabin without so much as a glance in the right direction.

The rickety home looked as though it had been abandoned for an entire year instead of one night. Its walls were worn yet sturdy after having obviously weathered more than its fair share of storms. The door never had a lock on it and opened on rusted hinges when Clint pushed on the chipped wood.

After walking inside, he found it easier to believe that the place had been left only about twelve hours ago. The chairs were positioned around the table in the same spot where they'd landed when their occupants had gotten up to leave. Tin pots and a few plates sat on top of a large cupboard that was half open and full of bread that had only recently gone stale. On the floor next to the fireplace was a rumpled blanket and a few stray pieces of clothing.

The bedroom was in slightly better order. A small wardrobe sat next to a cedar chest. Both were open with their contents in a state of disarray. Obviously, Kim had taken a few things as quickly as she could and left as fast as her feet could carry her. To further confirm her story, he spotted something lying on the bed.

Clint picked up the heavy hunting rifle and checked the barrel. It was loaded. Actually, the hammer was still cocked back and ready to be fired. Kim's fear hung onto the rifle just as tightly as her hands had the night before. Clint swore he could feel some of the woman's terror as she'd knelt on this bed and looked out the window.

Leaning over the bed, Clint took a look outside himself as he remembered the story she'd told him. After propping the rifle in a corner, he walked out the front door and traced the steps he imagined the killers to have taken.

Suddenly, he wondered if he didn't look like a fool for buying so completely into the story of a woman he hardly knew. Even though there was something in her voice that told him she had no reason to lie, the things she said just couldn't be true.

Could they?

Searching the ground for any trace of the killer's trail, Clint thought any trace of footsteps or anything else would have been lost in the thick mud and tangled weeds covering nearly every inch of ground in the area. Then, almost as if the bayou itself was trying to prove him wrong, Clint saw something that made his entire trip into the swamp worthwhile.

There at his feet, plain as day, was a set of tracks. Four, actually. And all of it was set in the bayou's mossy carpet like a message written in soft clay. All of it hardened by the Louisiana heat.

Two sets of footprints walked side by side with a pair of small ruts in between them. By the depth of the footprints, Clint could tell that they were left by big men who were dragging another smaller man. The shallow ruts were the size of a man's boot heels. Clint remembered Joseph was not a small man, but he wouldn't be much of a burden for the two that had left those tracks.

There was one more set of tracks overlaying the shallow ruts. Whoever that fourth man was, he'd walked behind the others. That was the one calling the shots, since he'd gotten the other two to carry Joseph's body.

Clint followed the tracks to where they ended in a small clearing behind the shack. Next to a wide stump with a woodchopping axe buried in it was a flattened out patch of weeds. Since the other three sets of footprints seemed to circle the flattened out patch, Clint figured they were looking down at Joseph's body. Squatting down to get a closer look at the ground, Clint eventually found an upturned patch of earth that had been blackened and slightly scorched.

There were two of those mounds which Clint instantly recognized as having been left by gunshots. Just like Kim had told him.

There was also plenty of blood around the flat patch that had nearly completely been soaked up by the absorbent earth.

Two things struck Clint as peculiar. First, the bullet markings were next to the flat patch of ground. If those shots had been the ones that had killed Joseph, the holes would have been dug right in the middle of his body's imprint. Second, the blood was also around the body and not a drop was spilled close enough to the bullet holes.

Now, Clint figured the killers might have moved Joseph's body as soon as they'd shot him, since they obviously moved the body at some point. But there should have been blood right on top of those bullet holes, or at least a hell of a lot closer to them than it was.

He thought about all of that on his walk back toward where Eclipse was tied. During the entire ride, he mulled over what he'd found and came away only with more questions.

The sun was setting by the time he rode back into Byers, so Clint tied the stallion up in front of the saloon next to the rest of the town's horses and stepped into the saloon to ask about getting a room for the night.

SEVEN

A pale, clammy hand wrapped around Joseph Terray's neck, squeezing just hard enough to bring bright, swirling blotches to his eyes. His body was a mass of bruised bones and screaming nerves. His skin felt like it was on fire and his ears still rang with the gunshots from the previous night.

When his senses cleared enough for him to get his bearings, Joseph tried to open his eyes and found even that slight motion wasn't worth the pain it caused. Instead, he shifted his body around in an attempt to get onto his knees. His hands searched the ground, but were buried in loose soil that squished wetly in his fist. When he tried to move his legs, he realized his whole body was wedged firmly in place and heavy soil pressed him down into the ground.

He could hear voices now. One was talking, although he couldn't quite hear what it was saying. One was laughing. When Joseph slipped in the loose earth and dropped face first to the ground, the laughter became almost hysterical.

Shaking his head, Joseph thought for a moment that his neck had been broken as sharp pain lanced up and down his spine. The sensations acted like a fire beneath him and Joseph struggled to his feet, opening his eyes to see where he was.

Dim light filtered through the familiar trees of the bayou. Stray beams hit him directly in the eyes, making it hard for him to see much besides shadows of different sizes and shapes. Besides the voices, he could hear the chirping of a thousand insects as well as the slosh of leathery bodies slipping through the water.

"Looks like he's finally awake," said the voice that had only just stopped laughing.

Footsteps squished in the mud until a thin figure blocked the sun from Joseph's eyes. Only then did he realize that the voices and the man looking at him were high above him, almost as though they were standing on top of a ladder or some kind of balcony. Then the smell hit him.

Turning, Joseph breathed in the stench of damp, moldy earth and could feel the cold wetness between his toes. He reached out to rub his eyes, but his hands were stopped by a solid wall of packed mud that was cool to the touch and warmed slightly the higher he forced his hands. He knew for sure at that moment that the other men didn't have to be on ladders to look down on him, not when he was standing in the narrow confines of a hole that had been dug deep into the floor of the bayou.

Joseph's first reaction was to scream. Spinning around on the balls of his feet, he searched frantically for a way out, only to see that the hole wasn't just a pit in the ground, but a grave. Just as wide as his shoulders and just long enough for him to lie down. His eyes made the measurements with desperate speed as his body began clawing at the wet walls of mud.

"It's sinkin' in, now isn't it?" asked the figure looming over him. "You wanna stay there, than you can lie down and we'll fill this hole back in."

"Oh, Jesus, no!" Joseph yelled before he could stop himself.

"Or," the voice continued, "you can take my hand and follow me back to the world of the living."

As if in answer to his prayers, a hand descended from the mess of light and shadows to hover over Joseph's head. When he reached up to take it, the hand pulled away and a sense of cold despair settled in Joseph's gut.

"I'll bring you back to life," the voice said. "I'll pull you out of the jaws of death itself, but it ain't free. You gotta promise me."

With every second that passed, Joseph swore the hole was getting smaller. Already, putrid moisture from the nearby swamp was leaking in and covering the tops of his boots. "Anything! Just get me out of here!"

The figure over him came a little closer. Then Joseph could

make out the form of Mason Rhyse kneeling on the edge of the grave. "You wanna live?"

"Yes. Please, God, I want to live."

"I ain't no God, but I can give ya what you're askin' for." Rhyse's voice was heavy beneath his Cajun accent, yet it sounded calm and compassionate. "You come back up here where the life is and you got ta pledge that life to me. I'm givin' it to ya, but only as a loan. If I decide to take it again, it'll be in a way that make that pit there look like a walk in the sun, eh? I take it back an' I'll send you down the long road to hell."

Joseph's mind was burning with all the horrific images that had been pounded into his head on Sunday mornings of what awaited the sinners. Rhyse's voice only added color to those thoughts, making him too scared to form another word. Instead, he waved his hand over his head in desperation until it was in Rhyse's firm grasp.

Although one of the bigger men could have done it much easier, it was Rhyse himself who grabbed hold of first one and then the other of Joseph's hands. He leaned back and planted his feet until they were rooted deep in the soft ground. Finally, Joseph emerged into the light and looked around the dirty swamp as if it was the promised land.

"Thank God," Joseph whispered as he dropped to his knees and turned his face to the setting sun. "Oh, thank God!"

"No," Rhyse said as he grabbed a handful of Joseph's hair and twisted his face until they were staring into each other's eyes. "Thank me!"

As darkness crept over the bayou, Mason Rhyse preached to his newly arisen. While Lovario and Stokes were out getting supplies, Rhyse talked endlessly until Joseph thought his ears were about to burst. And all the while, the skinny man in the dirty priest's collar mixed up a batch of sticky mud and chalk until it formed a thick, almost luminescent paste.

"You ain't had no life till this night," Rhyse said as he applied the paste to Joseph's face. "Up till now, you just been walkin' through every day, waiting for the end, just like all the others."

When his face was covered with the paste, Joseph could feel it hardening like a thin shell around his eyes and mouth, making it hard for him to part his lips. Even blinking was an effort once the thick concoction formed into an earthen crust.

And still, Rhyse kept preaching. "But all them others would'a been content to lie in their graves. Not you. Oh, not you. That's why I picked ya. That's why I picked all my men. We ain't many, but we got enough strength to roll over this land and take what we will."

Now, the balm was applied to Joseph's hands and forearms.

And still, Rhyse preached. "I took that strength from the devil and tore it from his hands! With those same hands that yanked you from the pit of hell just like you was yanked from your momma's belly."

When he was done, Joseph could see his skin gleaming in the darkness as if it had soaked up the moonlight the way a firefly soaked up the sun. Rhyse was almost out of the strange mixture and was smearing what was left onto Joseph's chest.

"You're mine, now," Rhyse stated. "You stay by my side and do as yer told, and I'll pass on the power from my hands into yours. I can bring all my men up from the ground, up above the living, and then up above the devil himself. I already beat that devil and I can teach you the same thing."

Rhyse's voice had become a droning buzz in Joseph's ears. Eventually, it was as though he wasn't hearing words, but absorbing the preacher's ideas. The smell of the swamp and the exhilaration of climbing out of his own grave made Joseph feel dizzy. Suddenly, everything Rhyse said made sense. After being talked to for so long, he'd lost track of time. Joseph felt beyond time and beyond death.

"There," Rhyse said with a quick, sharp tone. "Now you're ready to give them out there a taste of the grave."

Joseph got up and walked to a pool of murky water, broken only by the occasional reed poking its head above the surface. He looked into the moonlit water, feeling as though his joints had stiffened up worse than a dead man's. The face he saw in the water was no longer his own. Instead, it was a ghost looking back at him. A reflection not only of his visage, but of what was inside his brain.

After waking up in that hole in the ground and listening to Rhyse preach the sermon of death, Joseph was convinced that he'd been dead until he'd taken Rhyse's hand. Now, staring down at himself in the water, Joseph saw what he thought he should see: a dead man.

A ghost.

An unhappy spirit roaming the earth.

EIGHT

For the better part of a night, Clint wondered if he could get to sleep with all the strange images running through his head. First, there were the increasingly bizarre tales of what had happened to Joseph and those other two men who'd been taken by Mason Rhyse.

Then there were the tales about Rhyse, himself. Most of the stories began with him as a preacher in New Orleans who'd fallen from grace when he started worshipping the devil. Others say that Rhyse put more of his beliefs in voodoo than Christianity and still others said that Rhyse had killed his first man while still wearing his preacher's robes and therefore damned his soul.

Out of his vast experience with tall tales, Clint knew better than to trust anything at the more extreme ends of the spectrum. Rather, the truth always lay somewhere in the middle.

Finally, just on his way to the boardinghouse, Clint heard more than he'd ever wanted to hear about the local voodoo queens and how they'd either cursed or created the monster known as Mason Rhyse.

Now, Clint sat in his rented room in one of the unmarked buildings on Widest Street with his head propped up on a pair of pillows that weren't much more than sacks of tattered fluff and tried to make sense out of everything he'd seen and heard. Outside his window, the cicadas continued their endless chant and a few drunks fought loudly over who was going to be sick first. If he concentrated, Clint could still hear the music from the saloon.

Kim was singing again, her voice a sad wail in the night.

When he was finally able to think of nothing but the sound of her voice, Clint was able to drift off to sleep.

The next morning, Clint woke up to the smell of burning toast and black smoke that had the slightest scent of bacon mixed in.

"Breakfast's ready," came the voice of the woman who owned the boardinghouse. When Clint had seen her the night before, she'd reminded him of a schoolteacher, complete with the little round spectacles perched at the end of her nose. Black hair streaked with silver sat bundled at the back of her head and when she'd given him his room key, she'd looked him over from head to toe.

Clint had been so tired that he hadn't even noticed. Now, as his door inched open to let the black smoke drift in from the hall, he couldn't help but see her eyes gazing in hungrily at him. He'd instinctively sat up in bed and stretched his arms. As the sheet fell away from his body, Clint could hear a barely suppressed gasp from behind his door.

"I'm up, thank you," he said while gathering the sheets around him.

"Just thought you'd like some nice breakfast to get you going. I've put on coffee as well."

The stench drifting in from the kitchen was all he needed to swear off anything that had come from her oven, but the notion of a hot cup of coffee sounded perfect at the moment.

"I'm not hungry, but I think I could use . . ." Then the scent of burning coffee hit his nose like something that had come from the back end of a skunk. It made Clint choke on his words and wrinkle his nose in disgust.

"Could use what, dear?" the woman asked from where she'd been peeping through the door.

Clint maneuvered himself so he was sitting on the edge of the bed that faced away from the door. Luckily, his pants were on the floor there and he pulled them on without giving the boardinghouse's owner a free show.

"I think I could use a nice long walk to clear my head," Clint said. He tried to ignore his rumbling stomach and des-

perately tried to think of where he could go for a decent meal.
The saloon came to mind, so after pulling on his boots and
buttoning his shirt, Clint stepped out his door and walked
downstairs.

Careful to hold his breath as he walked past the kitchen,
Clint waved to the woman with the black and silver hair and
quickly stepped outside. For the first time since he'd arrived
in Byers, Clint actually welcomed the bitter, moldy smell of
the nearby swamp.

It was early in the morning and the streets were more full
than Clint had seen them since arriving in Byers. Mostly, cou-
ples were walking between the various stores with bundles in
their hands, going through their daily routines before heading
back to their homes on one of the little side streets or even
within the bayou itself.

The saloon was quiet except for the clinking of silverware
against plates as people at every table hungrily devoured their
food. Clint waited to see if anyone at a table was about to
leave, but didn't have any luck. When he stood at the bar, the
bartender came right over with a folded-up piece of paper and
pencil in hand.

"Here for breakfast?" he asked.

Clint looked one more time for a table, found nothing and
shrugged. "Yeah. Does your cook have any steaks?"

"She does, but only some that's left over from the last time
supplies came in from New Orleans."

"Which means?"

"Means I'd recommend anything but the steaks."

"Just give me a plate of whatever you'd recommend. And
coffee."

The coffee came first, piping hot and served in a mug that
still tasted like beer around the edges. When a plate was set
in front of him, it was covered with fried eggs, bacon, grits
and fresh corn bread. Clint devoured it all in minutes and
washed it down with the rich, dark coffee. By the time the
plate was taken from him, half the people in the saloon had
cleared out.

"So you're stayin' in town for a while?" the bartender asked.

"Yeah. I've got some business I need to tend to here.
Name's Clint."

The bartender nodded and held out his hand. "I'm Emmitt.

I hear you're lookin' to find the man that killed poor Joey Terray."

Clint shook the man's hand. "That's right. Have you got anything to tell me about what happened?"

"First thing is that you'd be a whole lot better off if you just let it go. Trust me, mister, this ain't nothin' you want to get mixed up in."

"Already heard that one," Clint said. "How about telling me another?"

"Ok, how about this? Man you're lookin' for is named Mason Rhyse. He's been making it his business to become something of a local terror in these here swamps. Been riding his men through from town to town, takin' what he wants and leavin' dead bodies in his path. I'm sure you heard'a him."

Clint nodded and said, "I don't know just how much of it I believe, but yeah, I've heard."

"Well, believe me when I tell you that Rhyse is a serious nightmare. He gets what he wants an' he don't even have to draw his gun, 'cause the folks around here are too scared to stand in his way. But he kills some of 'em anyways. He uses that voodoo curse of his like it was a gift."

As much as Clint hated to admit it, a lot of what Emmitt was saying made some sense. "What can you tell me about his . . . voodoo?"

"Not much. Not as much as Cleo, anyway."

"Cleo?"

"She's the town's medicine woman and voodoo priestess. She'll whip up anything from a love potion to a balm for poison ivy and she's the one that can tell you about voodoo."

"This ought to be good. Where do I find her?"

NINE

Madame Cleo lived in a two-story building at the other end of town. It took Clint about five minutes to walk all the way down Widest Street, find the correct side street and then locate the unmarked home of the local voodoo queen.

The building looked normal enough, complete with a pair of old rockers on a porch made of warped timber and a little balcony on the second level that was just big enough for one person to stand on. Just hearing the word "voodoo," Clint had expected strange dolls to be nailed on the door or even bizarre markings drawn on the walls. Instead, there was a mat in front of the door woven from straw and a pie cooling on the windowsill.

Clint stepped onto the porch and knocked on the door. Almost immediately, he could hear at least half a dozen cats answering the noise, meowing loudly inside.

"Oh, hush up now," came a muffled voice from inside the house.

The door opened, revealing a woman who was easily the width of its frame. She had smooth, dark black skin, stood about a foot and a half shorter than Clint and wore a light brown dress with a white apron tied around her waist. Her hair was tied back with a white handkerchief and as she spun around to keep one of her cats from skittering outside, Clint noticed that her hair went all the way down her back. Interspersed in the woman's thick mane were strands that had been

35

tightly braided and woven with beads. Wiping her hands on a
tattered rag, she looked up at Clint with a wide, beaming smile.
"What can Madame Cleo do for you?" she asked with a thick
Haitian accent.

"I need to see her. Is this the right place?"

"It certainly is the right place and you're seein' her now.
Please, come in." She stepped aside to let Clint pass, using her
foot to sweep away a pair of tan cats with patches of brown
on their fur.

The inside of the house smelled of incense and fresh lemon
pie. As he followed in Madame Cleo's footsteps, Clint could
also detect the slightest tinge of cigar smoke further inside.
The place had a homey feel, but seemed too nice to be in a
place like Byers. Lace doilies adorned rounded oak end tables.
Small, elegantly crafted paintings hung from the walls. Even
the carpet was exquisite and soft, except for all the cat hair
laced in between the fibers. Overall, not the kind of place he'd
expected to find in the middle of a swamp.

"I never seen you 'ere in town," Cleo said while leading
him to a parlor at the end of a small hallway.

Clint glanced up a narrow flight of stairs leading to another
little hall that was flooded with bright sunshine. "My name's
Clint Adams. I was on my way to Texas and decided to pass
through."

They were in the parlor now, which was lined with shelves
holding books, parchments, small wicker baskets, and jars con-
taining things that Clint could only identify with a lucky guess.
A round table sat in the center of the room, covered with what
appeared to be sailcloth that had been decorated with elaborate,
hand-drawn circular markings. There was also a window in
there, but it had been painted over with another strange symbol
that took up most of the pane. The hand-drawn symbol on the
glass seemed to bend the sunlight into strange patterns, making
the whole room appear to be tilted at odd angles.

"An' you come all 'dat way to talk to Cleo?"

"Not exactly. I was here to visit with a friend of mine.
Joseph Terray."

Cleo had waddled around the table and was about to pull
out her chair when she heard Joseph's name. Freezing for a
moment, she looked as though the words had touched her skin
like ice.

"He's a friend of yours?" she asked.

"Used to be. He was killed and I want to find the men who did it."

Now, Cleo sat in a simple mahogany chair that was obviously part of a set. She motioned for Clint to sit in a similar chair on the other side of the table, which he did.

"Your friend ain't dead," Cleo stated. "He been brought back from the other side by a man who keeps comp'ny with the likes of demons." Her voice had taken on a rich, almost musical quality while her hands had begun tracing over the patterns drawn onto the table. "He no longer dead, but he ain't no longer a man either."

Clint stared across the table at the short, black woman. He looked into her eyes, searching her face as if he was playing against her at a high-stakes game of poker. From what he could tell, Madame Cleo either believed what she was saying or she was a very good liar.

"Look, I don't believe in any of this," he said while motioning to the books and strange symbols surrounding them. "I was told that you could help me get a handle on Mason Rhyse. What I need from you is a way to track him down. Anything you can tell me would be appreciated, but I'm not here to have my fortune told or to hear ghost stories."

"Rhyse ain't no ghost. I could take care of a ghost from 'ere. He's much worse than any ghost. Much more powerful."

Deciding to play along with her, Clint folded his hands and put them in his lap so she could lean across and trace the designs in front of him. "All right. What is he?"

Cleo closed her eyes and began swaying back and forth in her chair. A low hum came from the back of her throat which hit the precise pitch to make Clint's eardrums start to vibrate. He shook his head slightly at the strange sensation just as a chorus of high-pitched voices began screeching behind him.

Turning, Clint saw a group of cats, well over a dozen in all, gathered at the threshold of the parlor. Not a single one of them set a paw inside the room.

Her chant died off until there was eventually a heavy silence in the air. Clint wasn't sure what to call it, but he got a peculiar feeling running from the base of his neck all the way down to his tailbone, which felt almost as though someone had run a cold finger down his back. Turning back to face Madame Cleo, he found her looking at him with the same open warmth that had made her face glow when she'd greeted him at the front door.

"Would you like some pie?" she asked from out of nowhere. "I jus' took it from the oven."

"What?" Clint asked, unable to hide his confusion.

"I find it's easier t'hear the bad things when you got somethin' sweet to balance it out. Balance is very important."

"Can you tell me about Rhyse or not?"

Cleo hesitated for a moment before leaning back in her chair, clasping her hands behind her head. "Whether you believe or not, Rhyse is a powerfully strong man. He not strong 'ere," she said while reaching across to jab a finger into Clint's bicep. "His strength come from 'ere." Now, she pointed to Clint's heart. "Rhyse's strength is the fear he can put into his followers as well as the people he hurts. It's a fear that grips a believer to their very core.

"Man who can wield that much fear don't need nothin' else. What is a weapon widout fear? That there," she said while pointing to the gun at Clint's side. "That can only kill a man. Rhyse can give you things worse than death."

For the better part of a minute, the only sound in the room was the uncomfortable mewing of a house full of cats.

"Sure y'don't want that pie?"

TEN

Joseph Terray felt the sun baking his face until the paste he wore started cracking and falling off in chunks. He, Rhyse and the other two men had been stalking through the swamps without so much as a word passing between them. The last time he'd heard another voice was in the morning when Rhyse had told him where they were going.

"There's a family lives down on the river 'bout four or five miles from here. They rich an' don't appreciate how lucky they are that I been leavin' them in peace for so long. We goin' to teach them a lesson."

Without much else to focus on during the long, hot walk, Joseph thought about those words as they rattled around inside his head. He tried to think about his wife and his existence before waking up in that pit, but all of that seemed so far behind him. All he had now was what Rhyse had given him. The only voice that made any sense came from Rhyse's mouth.

Joseph had gotten a taste of hell already and didn't want a full bite. If following Rhyse was what it took to stay out of the ground, then that's what Joseph decided he would do. As long as he roamed the world of the living, he knew he might someday see Kim's beautiful face again. All he had to do was keep moving.

The four painted men were heading northwest and the swamps were giving way to more solid ground. They'd been walking for hours and although none of the others showed any

39

signs of slowing down, Joseph felt his feet starting to ache and his body growing more and more sluggish.

Finally, he came to a stop, put his hands to his face and felt his muscles give out. Joseph toppled to the ground, hitting the mud with a solid thud.

Willie Stokes turned to look at him, his gaunt black face sticky with sweat and remnants of the muddy paste. Ed Lovario turned as well, walking swiftly over to where Joseph had fallen until he could bend down and grab hold of one of his hands.

Joseph took Lovario's hand and was hoisted to his feet. With a sudden snap of well-honed muscle, Lovario pulled Joseph closer and spoke in a voice that was barely loud enough to be heard. "Best keep on your feet," he said. "Rhyse don't tolerate nobody that slows him down. He'd kill ya quicker than he would a snake that crawled beneath his boot."

Joseph was surprised by the urgency in Lovario's voice. Until now, he'd thought he was the only one in the group who still had a shred of emotion left inside. Glancing over to Stokes, he saw the black man nod almost imperceptibly.

"What's goin' on back there?" Rhyse asked from the front of the line.

"Don't say nothin lest you have to," Lovario whispered while releasing Joseph's hand. "Jus' do what he says."

Rhyse stormed back to Joseph and Lovario, his heavy footsteps betraying a barely contained anger. "You better git movin'. We'll have plenty of time to sit back and enjoy the night when we've rolled through that house on the river. An' more time still when we've rolled through the county to collect our dues from people who ain't good enough to stand by our sides!"

With the bayou behind them, Rhyse and his men stalked up a path as it widened out to become a street. The town of Jespin used to be the home of Ed Lovario and when they were spotted by one of the local girls, an ear-piercing cry announced their arrival.

Jespin was home to a good number of families, the richest of whom had built a small plantation along the banks of the winding Mississippi. At the hottest part of the day, activity in the town had nearly ground to a stop. Besides the girl, who was now running as fast as she could away from Lovario, there were only two or three people to be seen.

The girl ran for one of the smaller buildings and was greeted by a pair of men with rifles in their hands. From where he was, Joseph couldn't hear what they were saying, but he could see by the way they gripped those guns that they meant to use them.

Rhyse motioned for Lovario to come up beside him. "This is your town," said the man in the dirty priest's collar. "This is your day. You know what to do."

The expression on Lovario's face was one of quiet surrender. He stepped forward as Rhyse signaled for the rest of them to stop and headed straight for the small group of locals gathering in the street.

One of them, a large man with the build of a petrified stump, met Lovario before he reached the other townspeople.

"That you, Ed?" he asked.

Lovario looked out with dead eyes as though there wasn't even a trace of a soul behind them. "Yeah, Frye. It's me."

"But it can't be. We all saw that one over there put a bullet into ya," Frye said while pointing over to Rhyse. "Ain't no man come back from that."

"I ain't a man no more."

The large man called Frye was built like a solid mass of muscle. When he turned to look back at his neighbors, the big man twisted at the waist. "They say I shouldn't waste my breath talkin' to a dead man. Old man Boyer told the whole town to keep an eye out for you after we found your empty grave. Said that if you come back, it was because we're cursed."

"You ain't the cursed one," Lovario said. He wanted to say more. Wanted to explain what'd been going on inside his head for the last few weeks and give Frye a message to send back to his family, especially to his daughter who'd screamed at the sight of her daddy only moments ago. Instead, he drew his face into a tight mask and reminded himself why he was there. "I'm the one holdin' the curse and them others with me are the same. We came back to claim our tribute. Let us have our due and we go back to where we came from. Stand in our way and when we kill ya, Rhyse ain't bringin' you back."

Lovario had spoken loud enough to be heard by the small

group huddled in front of the building behind Frye. When they heard Rhyse's name, they started whispering excitedly amongst themselves. The little girl began to cry.

Unable to watch for another moment, Lovario turned his back on Frye, the man who'd once been his closest friend, and walked back to stand beside Rhyse.

"They don't look ready to fill our collection plate," Rhyse said.

Lovario tried to keep his voice steady and quiet. "They know who you are, Rhyse. They know what they gotta do and they'll do it. Just tell me when to arrange for a collection and there won't be any trouble."

"What is all this?" Joseph asked when he saw that Stokes wasn't about to say anything. "What are we doing here?"

"We're taking our collection."

"Jus' like in church," Stokes said in a voice tainted by disgust.

Rhyse heard the other man's tone, but chose to ignore it for the moment. "That's right. I give life by pullin' bodies from the ground just as I save lives by keeping my spawn from taking it from those that still breathe. An' for that they gotta pay. They're willin' to hand over a lot more to a god they can't even see."

Turning to face the group of townspeople, Rhyse held his hands over his head which opened his long black coat to reveal the bits of holy clothing he wore. "You can see me! You can see what I done," he shouted while gesturing to the men everyone thought had been dead. "And if you don't pay, I'll be the last thing you ever see!"

ELEVEN

Clint sat in a small dining room with a fireplace taking up most of one wall and a stack of cabinets taking up another. The back door was held open by a string tied to the frame, which accounted for the ever-changing population of felines coming and going as they pleased. Outside, a delicate set of glass wind chimes clinked together to make a gentle song that drifted throughout most of Madame Cleo's house.

Once outside of her parlor, Cleo had transformed back into the kindly woman who doted on Clint like a long-lost grandson. Although he'd wanted her to continue with her story about Rhyse, she'd insisted on feeding him first. Now, she bustled about the kitchen and set a tall glass of milk in front of Clint.

"That's for you," she said. "An' now . . . where's that lemon pie?" Looking around, Cleo put her hands on her hips and must have looked past three other pies without giving them the slightest notice. "Monique!" she yelled in a voice that scattered the cats near the door. "Monique, where's that lemon pie? Find it an' serve our guest. He come a long way t'see us!"

Clint could hear the sound of light footsteps in the room directly over his head. They worked their way toward the front of the house and soon the stairs were creaking beneath someone's weight.

"You said to put the lemon pie in the front window so the cats wouldn't get to it," came a voice from the living room.

43

Madame Cleo shook her head and shrugged apologetically. "Children. You got any?"

"No," Clint smirked.

"Well they can be as much a curse as a blessing."

Just then, a slender black woman in her early twenties walked in holding the pie that Clint had seen when he'd first approached Cleo's house. She was a little taller than Cleo and had the same thin nose and wide eyes which gave both of their faces an exotic quality. On the younger one, however, the features were more pronounced and much more striking. When she walked across the room, her hips twitched like one of the several resident cats beneath a bright red and orange wrap tied around her waist.

Also like Cleo, the younger girl wore her hair braided with beads, only cut to just above her shoulders. Her breasts were full and round, bouncing perfectly with her every step. "What's our guest's name?" she asked in a voice that was just as smooth and rich as her chocolaty brown skin.

Clint's eyes lingered first on the generous curves of her body and then on the deep, earthy color of her eyes.

"I'm Clint Adams," he said while taking the pie from her hands and setting it on the table.

The girl smiled with soft, generous lips and quickly brushed her hands on her skirt before holding one out to him. "My name is Monique, in case you didn't hear my mother screaming it out to all of creation."

Clint took her hand, noticing how soft her skin was and how her grip was strong without being overpowering. She moved like an elemental part of her surroundings. Fresh and vibrant, yet also with the hint of there being plenty more going on beneath the surface. Monique's lips came together, turning her smile into a more sensual gesture as they pursed almost into a kiss.

"Your mother was just telling me about Mason Rhyse."

Her accent wasn't quite as strong as Cleo's, but it was enough to give her words an exotic flair. "Were you a friend of Joe's?"

"We only rode together once a year ago, but yes, I'd consider him a friend."

Monique walked to one of the cabinets and removed three plates and forks while Cleo dug into the pie with a large silver knife. As she moved about the kitchen, Clint couldn't help but notice the shift of Monique's hips and the way the beads in her hair brushed against the back of her neck.

"Lot of people in town been talking about Rhyse," Monique said. "Ever since last month when he came through demandin' money from anyone he could find."

Clint looked between the two women as the slice of pie was set in front of him. "Rhyse was here before?"

Nodding, Cleo sat down with her own helping. "He drifts through this whole area, orderin' them he sees to pay him tribute in return for him keepin' his curse out of their lives."

"Hasn't anyone refused to pay?"

"Sure they 'ave. An' I can think of three right offhand. Willie Stokes, Ed Lovario and your friend Joe Terray."

Clint nodded in appreciation of the first thing related to Rhyse that actually made some sort of sense. It was a simple protection scheme played by small-time gangs all over the country. The thugs would come around every so often to demand a tribute or they would punish the victims. Rhyse seemed to be taking a longer way about it, but there would be a lot less risk involved when none of his victims would even consider fighting back.

"So he travels from town to town, scaring people out of their money and killing the ones that don't pay?" he asked.

Monique nibbled at some of the pie on her plate. "Used to be that was all he did. That was back when it was just him and Pete Ballinger makin' the rounds."

"Who's Pete Ballinger?"

"Pete was a genuine man of the cloth," Cleo explained. "Unlike ol' Mista Rhyse. Pete worked a parish in the county northeast of here that Rhyse picked as a place to hide when he was runnin' from the law some five or six years ago. Way the story goes is that when the law did catch up to him, Rhyse took Pete with him as a hostage. They almost made it out of town before they both stopped a few bullets and down they went, priest and bandit both dead on the ground."

Picking up where her mother left off, Monique spoke in a voice that told Clint she didn't put much stock in what she was saying. "After they were buried, Rhyse and Father Pete were seen riding away into the bayou. And they haunted those swamps for years."

"You know how to get rid of a spirit?" Cleo asked. "You ask it to go. If it don't go, you try to force it to go. But the easiest way is to pay it to go."

Monique leaned forward, filling the air around Clint with her light, breezy scent. "You're not from around here, Clint, so you probably don't believe much of what we're saying. You look like a good, God-fearin' man. But every culture and every religion believes in some kind of tribute to their gods. The Greeks put money on the eyes of their dead to pay a ferryman to take them to the next world. Every church passes around a collection plate in the name of religious charity.

"Even superstitions revolve around appeasing the powers we don't understand. Why throw salt over your shoulder when you spill it? Why knock on wood? Why cross yourself or bless someone when they sneeze? It's all to make the spirits happy. That's why people pay Mason Rhyse. They don't want to cross paths with a dead man and he'll go away real fast if he gets what he wants."

"Well, he wants to take people away from their families and convince them they're dead," Clint pointed out. "To me, that's a whole lot different than asking for a few dollars."

"I agree," Monique said with a sharp nod. "All momma wants to do is brew her potions while I've been trying to get people to move against Rhyse. Any fool can see that he's not happy to stay in his swamps anymore."

"What do you mean?" Clint asked.

"Rhyse used to be a ghost story. Every couple of months someone would say they saw him. The money they paid wasn't much and they almost seemed to get a kick out of meeting a local legend. Rhyse has killed three times in as many months. Now, everyone has seen him and are scared to leave their homes at night. I'll bet he's feeding off of it. Maybe he lives off our fear."

Clint tried to keep his voice neutral when he asked his next question. "So you think he's dead too?"

"I was at Willie Stokes's funeral, Clint. I saw his body and I blessed it for his last journey and then I saw him standing next to a man who's supposed to be a ghost. What should I think?"

"What if I could prove that Joseph Terray hadn't been shot the other night?" Clint asked.

Monique was still leaning forward. Her eyes searched Clint's face for any reason to doubt his words, but could find none. She started to say something, stopped, and then sat back to think.

Surprisingly, it was Madame Cleo who said what Clint had wanted to hear. "You prove that an' we all sleep better at night. What we need is for someone to shake the fear he's been buildin'."

Pointing to the older woman, Clint said, "That's exactly right."

"But how much proof do you need?" Cleo asked. "How much convincin' will it take for you to take the chance of tanglin' with a monster who can't be killed?" She leaned forward, her face suddenly taking on the tense seriousness she'd shown in her parlor. "Do you have enough faith to look the devil in the eyes without blinkin'?"

Clint couldn't answer right away.

"Magic is all about lookin' the wrong way at the right time," Cleo said softly. "You remember that if you decide to face him down."

TWELVE

Madame Cleo spent the next several minutes in the kitchen mixing up a balm to ward against the will of evil men. While she shuffled back and forth between there and her parlor in search of certain ingredients, Monique took Clint outside to pick a specially grown weed from an impressive herb garden.

"So are you learning your mother's craft?" Clint asked.

Monique laughed and stooped down to pull out a handful of leaves. "You say that like I'm learning how to cheat at cards. She helps a lot of people in this town. In fact, people come from lots of other towns to get her medicines."

"Have you learned how to curse anyone yet?"

Looking up to stare him straight in the eyes, she turned the corners of her mouth down until she was wearing her mother's dead-serious expression. "Of course I have. An' I wouldn't step under no ladders if I were you."

Clint thought she was serious for about a second and a half. Finally, they both broke out into laughter.

"Sorry about that, Monique. It's just that I'm used to getting a more practical kind of help. I didn't mean to insult you."

"I've heard a lot worse from some people and I'd much rather be called impractical than a witch any day. But something does strike me as odd."

"What's that?"

"How come you're still standing around here if you don't think we can be of any help to you? I'm sure you can think of a lot better ways to spend your time than wait for my mother to make something you'll probably throw away or feed to your horse when you leave here."

"Actually, I've gotten a lot of information about Rhyse. After listening to your stories, I almost feel as though I know him."

Monique sorted through some roots that she'd pulled from the ground, examining each one while turning them over in her hands. "We can help you with a lot more than that."

Clint knelt down to her level. Besides making it easier to talk, he enjoyed being that little bit closer to her smooth, fragrant skin. "I may not believe that Rhyse is dead, but I'm sure he's dangerous."

"His biggest tool is fear. He uses people's fear and superstitions about spirits and voodoo to make them too scared to resist him. My mother is known throughout this state for her charms. She's a voodoo queen, which means she can start a little fear of her own, only directed at Rhyse and his men."

Clint was impressed. "That's not a bad idea. She really could do that?"

Pausing for a second, Monique stood up and looked down at Clint with fiery determination in her eyes. "So could I."

Before Clint could respond, the back door flew open to allow Madame Cleo and a trio of cats to come outside. "Monique, bring in 'dem roots so I can get this finished for the man!"

Monique started to walk toward the door, but lingered next to Clint, her hand drifting to touch his. "I knew Joseph Terray, too. And I've been watching people come in here to beg my mother for some way to lift the curse of Mason Rhyse. I'm not the type to beg, but I am askin' you. Please let me help you. I can even be a guide through the bayou if that's all you need, but I know I can do a lot more for you than that."

The feel of her warm touch on his skin sent a surge through Clint's system. "Do you know where I can find Rhyse or where he may be headed?"

"Monique!" Cleo shouted. "I said get over here!"

"Rhyse has a pattern," Monique quickly said. "Just like any spirit, but I need more time to tell you about it. Where can I find you?"

"The saloon."

"Then I'll meet you over there in a few hours. She'll be wanting me to bring this over to you when she's finished, anyway."

Clint squeezed her hand without even thinking about it. "Thank you, Monique."

"Don't thank me yet. Wait till you see what I can do."

Waiting until she'd gone inside, Clint whispered to himself, "I can only imagine."

Joseph Terray stood watch outside the camp Rhyse had allowed them to set up outside of Jespin. He'd been so disoriented the night before that Joseph had barely known which direction the men were leading him. Now, after he'd had a chance to look around a bit, he knew where he was and how far away he'd wandered from his beloved Kim.

Joseph wondered what she was doing right then. He hoped she was praying for him because he would need all the help he could get after the darkness had rolled back over the horizon. Rhyse was sitting with his back to him, talking in quick whispers to Stokes and Lovario. Although Joseph didn't know what the plan was, exactly, he did know that they would be moving in and taking prisoners whether the townspeople decided to pay or not.

Looking up at the bright Louisiana sky, Joseph began thinking of a way to put some distance between himself and these other men. For a man that was supposed to be dead, Joseph was feeling awful tired. Somehow, that just didn't seem right.

Then, almost as if he'd sensed Joseph's thoughts, Rhyse made his way back to his side and started in on his preaching. Out came the flask from within Rhyse's undertaker coat and then came a toast.

"To a profitable night," Rhyse said while handing Joseph the flask. "And to the harvester of souls."

Joseph couldn't taste the whiskey as he tossed it back and tried not to look at the cold eyes staring at him. He just looked at the sky and imagined Kim's beautiful voice. "Pray for me," he whispered.

THIRTEEN

Clint headed back across town toward the saloon. When he got there, the saloon was just over half full of people, most of whom were nursing mugs of dirty beer while swapping stories with their neighbors. Clint walked up to the bar and waved for Emmitt to join him.

"You been to see Miss Cleo?" the barkeep asked.

"Yeah. She sure likes those cats, doesn't she?"

Emmitt laughed. "She does at that. But it's not like she got much of a choice. Any cat that come near this town winds up at that house of hers. Almost like they think she's the only one who's good enough to visit."

Clint put that little tidbit in his brain next to all the others regarding the voodoo woman. He wasn't quite a believer in her magic, but he couldn't rightly explain it yet either. "What about her daughter? Is she following in her mother's footsteps?"

"Oh, Monique ain't quite ready for all that, but she's on her way. I had a boil on my arm," Emmitt said as he began rolling up his sleeve. "Size of a grape and she—"

"That's all right. I'll take your word for it. What I meant was does she know her business? Does she travel much outside of Byers?"

Emmitt rolled his eyes in his head as though the answer was written on the inside of his forehead's bony ridge. "Uh, sure she travels. She's got to since Madame Cleo started gettin' up

51

in years. Any time someone from another town needs their help, it's Miss Monique that heads out there."

As far as sources of information, Clint normally didn't like going to practitioners of hokey con games or spiritualists. More often than not, those types were only interested in making what they did look good enough to keep the suckers lining up at their doors. But Cleo and Monique seemed different. Inside, Clint felt they could be trusted, but he needed a little more convincing.

"Monique told me about the man I'm after," Clint said. "I just wanted to know how reliable she was before I go off on some wild-goose chase."

"You listen to whatever she tell ya, mister. She ain't got no reason to lie."

"I guess not," Clint said, even though he could think of plenty of reasons. Then again, it could also be that his years had made him a little too paranoid for his own good.

"What can you tell me about Mason Rhyse, Emmitt?"

Suddenly, the entire saloon went dead quiet. The boisterous conversations, rowdy jokes and even the scattered chat sessions all came to a stop. Every eye in the place turned toward Clint.

One of the old-timers sitting at the other end of the bar ground his few rotting teeth together while pointing a bony finger in Clint's direction. "Ain't no good sayin' that name in here. What you tryin' t'do boy? You tryin' to ruin things for all of us?"

Reaching out with a firm hand, Emmitt grabbed Clint's arm and spun him toward the door. "I think it's time for you to leave," he said while walking around the bar. "Come on, now before you do any more damage."

At first, Clint was going to protest. Then he saw the insistent look in Emmitt's eyes. There wasn't as much threat in his expression as there was urgency. And when Emmitt waved quickly for him to follow, Clint knew he wasn't getting kicked out so much as he was being moved away from the others.

The hand on Clint's elbow was trying to look firm, but was only strong enough to guide him around a corner and away from the saloon's front door. As soon as they were both standing on a small side street which led between a pair of split-level shacks, Emmitt released Clint's arm and backed off.

"Sorry about that, mister," Emmitt said in the voice of a kid expecting the strap to fall at any moment.

"It's all right. And please call me Clint."

"I jus' needed to get you outta there so we could finish what we was sayin'. They're too suspicious in there to even mention Rhyse's name anymore . . . especially after what happened."

"Actually, I can't really blame them for that."

Relieved, Emmitt took out papers and a bag of tobacco from his shirt pocket and began nervously rolling himself a cigarette. "I used to have a place up in Jespin, a town not too far from here where the swamps ain't so damn thick. Nice place. Helluva lot nicer than this, anyway." He paused to lick the edge of the rolled-up paper and seal the tobacco inside. It took him three tries.

"I was there a few months ago when Mason Rhyse came ridin' through town lookin' for his tribute," Emmitt continued. "Now, normally, he was satisfied with a few dollars and some food. Folks would leave it out on their doorsteps or in the graveyard, more for good luck than anythin' else. They'd wake up the next mornin' and it'd be gone. Some would say they saw the dead men makin' the collection.

"That last time, though, Rhyse came through like a thunderstorm. He was shootin' folks up and all his men were cuttin' them down. Some of them that rode with him carried blades longer than yer arm."

"How many were there?" Clint asked.

"At least six or seven."

"I thought there were only two or three."

"Well, back then, Rhyse and his men could afford to travel in a bigger pack. Until he got cocky."

"So you don't believe all the stories about Rhyse either?" Clint asked.

Emmitt's brow furrowed in thought. His eyes searched around for any sign of someone else listening to them, even though there was obviously nobody around. "I used to. But some of us back in Jespin fought back against Rhyse's killers. Got in a few lucky shots, too. Dead men don't bleed like they did when we got in our licks, mister. And they went down screamin' like anyone else would'a after takin' a shot to the chest."

"But Rhyse got away?"

Nodding, Emmitt took a long draw off his cigarette. "Yeah. After he took the bodies of his men back to the swamps, he came back with only one other man, and they wasn't like before."

"What do you mean?"

"They was pale," Emmitt said while moving a hand over his own face. "Their skin was fallin' off their bones and left behind somethin' that looked like it had been dug up outta the ground. When they came back, we was all too scared to fight back much. That's when he took Eddie Lovario."

"That's one of the men riding with Rhyse now."

"Yep. He came into Eddie's house, tied up his wife and little girl so's they could watch as they put a bullet into Eddie and left him for dead."

"Let me guess," Clint said. "The body was gone before they could bury him?"

"That's right. Now, we all seen Eddie at least once. He look like Rhyse now. Pale, rottin' away, but still walking. Bad luck to lay eyes on 'em or even talk about 'em. They say they's all cursed."

Clint was thinking about what he'd found at Joseph's home, but didn't want to get into a long discussion about disproving a ghost story at the moment. He knew it would take less evidence to swing a jury than it would to get superstitious people to change their beliefs. So for the moment, he nodded and took in Emmitt's story.

"You was askin' me about Miss Monique," Emmitt said. "She's got a good head on her shoulders. She's helped a lot of people and, just between you and me, she don't believe what they say about Rhyse either. She told me after they found Joey that Rhyse ain't nothin' but a man with a murderous heart."

Clint shook Emmitt's hand while placing a few coins into the barkeep's palm. "Thanks for your time. I sure do appreciate it."

"You're still welcome in my place," he said. "But just do me a favor if you don't mind."

"What's that?"

"At least make like I brought you out here to keep you in line. I need to keep my end up and all."

"No problem, Emmitt," Clint said as he walked from the

side street. Once he got in front of the saloon, he added in a slightly raised voice, "And I hope I didn't cause you any harm for stepping out of line."

Emmitt was standing in the open door now, with one foot inside the saloon. "Jus' don't ever let it happen again!"

Clint laughed to himself and started walking toward the post where Eclipse was tied. To his surprise, he found Monique already there, gently stroking the stallion's mane.

"I couldn't wait," she said. "We need to do something before anyone else gets hurt."

FOURTEEN

It took less than half an hour for Clint to find himself riding Eclipse through a tangled path leading to the town of Jespin. Behind him, Monique was sitting with her arms wrapped tightly around Clint's midsection and her face pressed close against his neck. When he'd seen her in front of the saloon, all she would tell them was that they needed to head out and that she would explain along the way.

After Eclipse had fallen into a steady gallop on the firm ground skirting the bayou, Clint turned to get a look at Monique. "Are you ready to start explaining this to me," he asked, "or do I have to wait until we get to wherever we're going?"

"I told you we're going to Jespin."

"I'll need more than that or I'll turn right back around."

"I think that's where Rhyse was headed. Now that he's got another man to follow him, he'll be looking for some money to fund his next job."

"You talk about him like he's not the spirit of the swamps or whatever the rest of the people around here want to call him. I'd have thought that you and your mother would be more interested in keeping those people afraid of Rhyse so they would come to you more often for help."

"Is that what you think?" she asked with a definite edge in her voice.

"Maybe."

Monique reached forward, snatched the reins from Clint's

hands and drew Eclipse to a stop. The Darley Arabian didn't appreciate the sudden halt, but eventually complied. As soon as she was able, Monique hopped down to the ground and stepped around to stare up at Clint with her hands set firmly on her hips.

After calming the horse, Clint swung his leg over the saddle and dismounted also. "I wouldn't recommend you trying that again, or you'll find yourself walking back to town. Gators or not!"

Ignoring him, Monique leaned forward until she was practically nose to nose with Clint. "Are you accusing me and my mother of something, Mister Adams? Because if that's the case, I'd like you to just come right out and say it."

"Look, I'm no believer in all this walking dead talk and I don't take kindly to those who take advantage of others' beliefs."

"You think I'm lying to you? You think me and my mother are out to cheat people like some kind of snake oil salesman?"

Clint held his ground in front of the angry young woman. "I've met my fair share of cheats and the first thing they all do is get people to believe in whatever it is they're saying. After that, it's just a matter of asking for the cash."

"Did we ever ask for your money? Did we ever ask you to believe what we were telling you?"

"I'm not the one who paid for that big house of yours that makes every other place in town look like rotten shacks. I guess the voodoo spells and potions you cook up are worth everyone's hard-earned money?"

Monique started to reply and a hint of red colored her dark complexion, but then she seemed to think twice. Slowly, she took a step back and a smile drifted across her face. "You're a very careful man, Clint. You think that by getting me all upset, I'd slip and say something that I'd regret?"

Studying her face, Clint watched Monique's expression turn from angry to suspicious and eventually back to calm. Not once did she show the look of guilt that tainted the smiles of a liar. He'd been hoping that she wasn't trying to lie to him or lead him astray for whatever reason, but he knew better than to rely on hope alone.

"I had to be sure, Monique."

Turning her back on Clint, Monique took a few steps off

the trail before turning back to face him. Now, she wore a wide, beautiful smile that seemed to brighten her entire face. "You're not used to taking a lot on faith, are you?"

"Faith does a man wonders in church, but can cause a lot of trouble outside of it."

"Well, you're more right than you know. Rhyse twists people's faith until it becomes his weapon. And he uses that weapon well enough to dodge bullets before they're even fired at him."

"I talked to Emmitt and he told me about what happened in Jespin. Is that why we're headed that way?"

Monique nodded. "In a way. I do a lot of traveling in my mother's name, making deliveries and practicing our craft in nearby towns. Before Rhyse came to Byers, he passed through a town south of here. Jespin is next in line."

"Now that's reasoning I can follow," Clint said. Stepping closer to her, he put his hands on her shoulders and looked into Monique's eyes. "Maybe you shouldn't come with me. If Rhyse is in Jespin, then things may get pretty rough."

Turning her head down, Monique took a deep breath and reached up to put her hands on top of Clint's. When she looked back up, the beads in her hair rattled together to make a sound similar to pearls being poured from one hand to another. "My mother and I are the closest thing this area has to a real doctor. On top of that, we hear their confessions, steer them toward love, bless their children and pray to the spirits for them to have a better life. We care for everyone we help, Clint, and Rhyse is using our same beliefs to cause pain. I can't stand by and watch something like that. Please don't ask me to. That would be like askin' a priest to watch a thief steal from the poor box."

Clint understood perfectly what Monique was saying. Although he didn't like the idea of her tagging along, he couldn't expect her to stay behind. Even if he didn't take her, he knew she would find her way to Jespin on her own.

"All right," he said. "But only on one condition. You've got to promise me to do what I tell you when I tell you. Because if things do go bad, you'll be better off letting me handle them."

"Ok. But you've got to listen to me when we deal with things I know about. Even if they seem strange to you."

"Fair enough," Clint agreed as he mounted up. Reaching down with one hand, he helped Monique back into the saddle. As Eclipse started running, Clint could feel her holding on to him a little tighter, her hands kneading the muscles in his chest.

FIFTEEN

The ride to Jespin would have taken a lot longer if Eclipse hadn't been tied to a post for the better part of a day and was now raring for some exercise. Feeling the stallion move and listening to its gruff breathing, Clint decided there had to be a better place to keep Eclipse instead of the front of a saloon. For now, however, the Darley Arabian's restlessness served a purpose and they were in sight of Jespin in record time.

Clint drew to a stop once he was within the town limits and took a look around. There wasn't any immediate sign of trouble, but he knew that wasn't any reason to relax his guard. Monique was still hanging on tightly and he could sense more urgency in the young woman's embrace.

"Everything looks quiet for now," he said.

"That's because Rhyse does most of his business at night," she said while scanning the horizon. "We've got a few hours yet before he'll be making any moves."

"Are you sure about that?"

"No."

"Then it's time for you to start keeping that promise you made," Clint said while turning to help Monique down from the saddle. "I'll scout things out real quickly while you stay here in town. Maybe you can get some information as to what Rhyse might have planned."

"See that building over there?" she asked while pointing to a squat structure covered in chipped green paint. "I'll meet

60

you there in two hours. Will that give you enough time?"

"Plenty." He watched as Monique turned and started walking for one of the busier streets. "Be careful," he called to her back.

With a quick wave over her shoulder, Monique wished him well before stepping onto the boardwalk lining the street. Clint turned Eclipse back toward the edge of town and began circling the perimeter.

Jespin turned out to be about twice the size of Byers, with plenty of well-built homes forming a circle around the town's limits. The Mississippi itself made up Jespin's eastern border and three of the estates had their own small docks, but nothing large enough to accommodate anything bigger than a rowboat.

Eclipse seemed to linger around a decent livery which gave off the smell of fresh hay and other horses. With a snap of the reins, Clint pressed on and circled back into town with plenty of time to spare.

While definitely larger than Byers, Jespin wasn't a big town by any stretch of the imagination. It had a livery, two saloons and several stores, which made Clint certain he'd been right in his guess about trade being the main source of the town's income. Also, there were at least three hotels for the merchants that came along with the cargo boats floating down the Mississippi.

As he rode through the town, scouting out the lay of the land, Clint felt like there was something he'd missed on his patrol. Something stuck in the back of his mind like a little splinter in his hatband that was just sharp enough to let him know it was there. He thought about what he'd seen and what he was looking for. When he'd just about finished his tour of Jespin, Clint realized what it was that had been bothering him so much.

Checking his pocket watch, he saw that he had just over half an hour before he was supposed to meet Monique. Eclipse didn't need much urging before the stallion was trotting out of town and heading back toward the river at a full gallop. They were soon riding back to the second estate he'd seen which had its own fenced-in property.

Although he'd seen plenty of locals going about their business as he'd made his rounds, Clint hadn't realized right away just how many people were milling on the grounds of this particular home. To check out his theory, Clint rode up to the house, which was a fine estate about three quarters the size of a plantation house, and counted the men walking around the land.

It only took him about a minute to spot ten men, all armed with rifles or shotguns, pacing in front of the house like they were guarding a prison. The only question on Clint's mind was whether those men were keeping someone in or out. He figured there was one quick way to find his answer, but before he started asking any questions, Clint decided to keep his appointment with Monique on schedule and head back into town.

Besides, she might have found out enough to keep him from revealing why he was there to anyone who might pass along the information to Rhyse.

On the way back, he kept his eyes out for other armed men guarding any of the other homes or businesses. The rest of the town seemed normal and by the time Clint made it back to the building Monique had shown him, the sun was beginning to slip out of sight beneath the western horizon.

Monique was standing outside, waiting for him with her hands wrapped tightly around her. The wind was becoming cooler, but not nearly cool enough to give the chill that hung over her face and brought her shoulders up close to her ears. When he brought Eclipse to a stop, Clint saw that her dark skin had lost some of its color and her eyes gave away the trouble in her heart.

"Looks like I should have stayed with you," Clint said as he extended a hand to help her climb into the saddle behind him. "Are you all right?"

"I'm fine, Clint. Just get me away from that place."

They rode down the street and turned a corner. Then, with the building out of sight, Clint dismounted and helped Monique down as well. They were in front of a row of small shops and a restaurant that was teeming with the dinner rush. After tying off Eclipse, Clint led Monique into the restaurant and sat down at a table in the corner. He ordered them both some water and waited until she'd had a drink before checking on her again.

"Are you all right?" he asked a second time.

"I saw him, Clint."

"Who? Rhyse?"

She took another sip of water and shook her head. "No, I saw Willie Stokes."

"He's one of Rhyse's men, right? The one that used to live in Byers?"

"That's right."

"Where was he?"

"I was visiting with a family I'd come to visit last week. They've got a sick little boy and I wanted to check on him while I was here. They also told me about what had happened the other night . . ." Her words trailed off and her color paled half a shade more. Closing her eyes, Monique took another sip of water.

Clint didn't need for her to say the man's name to know who she was thinking about. "How many did Rhyse have with him?"

"Three. They said they come for their tribute and that they were going to take someone with them."

Nodding, Clint pictured the estate he'd found that had been turned into an armed barracks. "Where did you see Stokes?"

"He was there . . ." she said softly. "There when I closed my eyes, but gone when I opened them. His face was painted white and his eyes were sad."

"Wait a minute. You saw him in a vision?"

She nodded. "I know it was true because I talked to plenty of others while you were gone. They all say the same thing." Monique brought the cup of water to her lips and drained it all. "They said Rhyse is coming tonight . . . and he wants blood as his tribute."

SIXTEEN

After they'd eaten, Clint and Monique moved to the saloon so they could wait for the ghost riders over a cold drink. Surprisingly, the beer he ordered was actually pretty good. Monique had one as well, but hardly got a chance to drink it before she was bombarded with townspeople coming to her with any number of problems.

People of all shapes, sizes, ages and gender came to Monique as word spread throughout Jespin that she was in town. Clint sat back and watched as the young lady held court, dispensing everything from marital advice to remedies for a fever. He couldn't help but be impressed by the way she held herself and refused all the payment that was offered in return for her time.

"How could you have ever learned so much?" Clint asked once there was a lull in the flow of visitors. "I mean, how much of that do you just make up on the spot?"

Monique laughed and patted the back of his hand. "I've been learnin' since I could understand a word my mother was saying. I told you we see people from all around and for the last few years, I've been going to those that can't come to us."

"I guess when I think of voodoo, I think of people screaming and making strange little dolls with pins in their chests."

Pausing for a second, Monique took a sip of her beer before looking down at the table. "There's some of that too."

Before Clint could ask her more, the door to the saloon was

flung open and a pair of small children came running inside. They were two little girls wearing calico dresses and shoes with holes in the toes. One had dark red hair cut just above her ears while the other wore hers in long pigtails that were bright blonde. Both of them were breathing heavily with their faces turning beet red.

Ignoring the adults asking them what they were there for, both girls looked hurriedly around the room until they spotted what they were after. With the speed of frightened rodents, the children skittered around the bar, between the drinkers standing there and around the tables until they stood between Clint and Monique.

"What is it, children?" Monique asked while reaching out to rub the tops of their heads.

Neither of the girls could have been a day over six, but they had enough fear in their eyes to fill up several lifetimes. "Our pa sent us for you," the little blonde said excitedly. "He tol' us that you'd be here and that we needed to come get you."

The redhead swiveled around like a puppet on a stick until she was looking up at Clint. She raised a little hand to point at him, nearly jabbing his nose. "And him. Pa says you should come too."

This time, Clint reached out to try and soothe the girls. He put a hand on the redhead's shoulder and looked down into her cute, dirt-smudged face. "What's the matter? Is someone in trouble?"

Both of the girls seemed to be gathering what little courage their bodies could muster. Finally, their lips pursed as if in a last ditch effort to hold back their words before they came slipping out.

"He's here," they both said in unison.

Clint was on his feet and out of the saloon in a rush with Monique trailing right behind him. The girls stayed in the doorway, peeking around from either side to watch the excitement that was going to follow their announcement. The remaining people that had been inside the saloon wanted to take a look outside as well, but were not quite up to getting themselves through the door.

Outside, Clint stood waiting for any sign of Mason Rhyse and his men. After all he'd heard about them, even he half expected to see something fresh from a nightmare come thundering up to the saloon on a steed made of smoke.

The sound of hooves echoed off the buildings and bounced down the street. Since there wasn't much activity in town after dark, the horses sounded even louder than normal. What remained of the sunlight was nothing but an orange smudge in the distance, which gave the whole scene a fiery tint that made the approaching riders seem otherworldly and vaguely sinister.

Clint could see three of them, riding side by side to take up the entire street. They were arranged so that the two bigger men rode on either side of the smaller one. If he'd learned anything from his experience, Clint figured the smaller one to be Rhyse. It always worked out that the smaller fellas were the meanest. They probably had something more to prove.

"What should we do, Miss Monique?" asked one of the townspeople behind Clint.

Not wanting to take his eyes off the approaching men, Clint held his ground and spoke loud enough to be heard without needing to turn around. "Any of you men that are armed stay outside with me."

A man Clint had seen in the saloon stepped up next to him. He looked to be in his mid-fifties and was cradling a shotgun in the crook of his arm. "We ain't the killin' sort, mister. Hell, I ain't fired this gun at nothin' but quail."

The riders were a block away now.

"It doesn't matter how good of a shot you are," Clint said. "All I need is for those men to see that I'm not alone out here. If any shooting starts, just point that thing in the right direction if you pull the trigger. Otherwise, get down and stay out of my way."

Slowing their horses to a walk, the riders approached the saloon. Now, Clint could see the pale faces that almost glowed in the fading light. Their skin seemed thick and milky, hanging ghostlike around dark, sunken eyes.

Clint took a quick glance behind him, just to make sure that Monique was safely tucked away somewhere. Only then did he realize that there wasn't one, but three other men standing at his side. Every one of them had a shotgun or rifle held in their arms. Turning his attention to the riders as they pulled to a stop in front of him, Clint grew anxious to bring all of Rhyse's plans to a stop.

For a few seconds, all that could be heard was the deep

rumble of the horses' breathing. Their reins jerked at the bits in their mouths, causing them to pull their heads around and snort loudly. In the muggy heat, the animals blew thick clouds of steam from their nostrils and bared their teeth.

Clint could hear voices coming from the group, but couldn't quite make out who was speaking. When he looked to his sides to double-check his backup, he saw that the townspeople holding the shotguns looked as though they were seeing the arrival of the devil himself. They were so transfixed by Rhyse that they'd all but forgotten about the guns in their possession.

Now, a voice from the group of riders made itself be heard above everything else. "Too late to stand up and fight now," it said. "Pay my tribute or die slow and messy."

SEVENTEEN

"So you're the dead men I've been hearing so much about?" Clint asked. His eyes were focused on the man in the middle who sat his horse as if he could ride that animal from one end of the globe to another. The men on either side looked ready to fight, but not anxious for it.

Mason Rhyse glowered down at the gathering of townspeople. In particular, he paid close attention to the man who'd just spoken. "I've never seen you before," Rhyse said. "What's your name?"

Clint shrugged. "Since you're not going to be around here much longer, I don't see that my name really matters all that much."

"Surely you know me. I'll bet you know my men. Hell, I'd even wager that these scared folks here have told you a whole lot about us. And you want to know something else? They've got good reason to be scared."

Stepping forward, Clint reached out until he could feel the muzzle of Rhyse's horse in the palm of his hand. The animal's nose was hot and it pushed its breath out in forceful bursts. "This animal feels alive enough to me," Clint said. "And my wager is that you're just as alive as this horse."

Clint looked up, first into the face of the big man to Rhyse's left and then up at Rhyse himself. "You've made a living off of scaring these people and that seems yellow enough to me.

But when you start killing them, I take offense. Especially when you start killing friends of mine."

Snapping his horse to attention, Rhyse twitched a spur into his animal's side to startle it just enough to take a bite at Clint's hand. Its teeth snapped shut on empty air as Clint whipped his hand away with an easy speed. The display didn't even make Clint back up a step, but Rhyse grinned as though his little prank had been a complete success.

"I ain't killed nobody, mister," Rhyse said. "Y'see this?" Pointing to the priest's collar around his neck, the scrawny man with the pale skin tugged at it as if the scrap of material had a power all its own. "This here makes me a man of the spirits. I feel that connection to the almighty and it gives me the power of death and everything that comes after."

Suddenly, Clint grabbed hold of the rein to Rhyse's horse. With a quick pull, he yanked them from the rider's hand as the animal started to whinny in protest. "You do too much talking to be a dangerous man," Clint said right before he bunched up the leather straps and lashed out to slap them across Rhyse's face.

The rider's head snapped back and the sound of the stinging slap echoed down the street. Clint had already stepped back to join the crowd with a grim smile on his face. Almost immediately, Monique was beside him.

"What are you doing?" she whispered in his ear.

Clint replied without taking his eyes away from the pale men, speaking just loud enough for her to hear. "I'm showing these people that these men aren't all-powerful. They're here to fight, so I'd rather force their hand and get it over with than stand here talking all night. Besides, those other two next to Rhyse look like they don't want to be here at all."

Rhyse had turned his horse around after calming it down and was leaning in close to his men. He whispered orders first at one and then at the other before finally swinging himself out of the saddle completely. He dropped to the ground and landed with both feet planted firmly in the mud. Walking forward, Rhyse didn't once look back to his men who both stayed atop their horses.

When he got close enough, Clint could see the mark on Rhyse's face where the strap had hit him. Just as he'd thought, the pale covering of dead skin was nothing but a shell that had chipped away beneath the strap. Clint wasn't normally one to provoke a man, but he needed to chip away at the illusion Rhyse had created and the strap had done a nice job of doing just that.

Rhyse walked up until he was within arm's reach of Clint, stopped, and then glared at every set of eyes that were turned in his direction.

"Looks like your makeup is falling off," Clint said to draw attention to the flaw in Rhyse's facade.

There were a few grumbled words among the men in the front of the saloon, but before much else could be said, Rhyse reached up and tore a chunk of the crusted mud from where it had been chipped off across his cheek.

"You want a trophy?" Rhyse asked in a voice that trembled with rage. "You want to tempt death? You want to see the face of the reaper?" With each question, Rhyse made his voice louder and louder until he finally screamed, "You want to peel away my flesh until you can stare the devil in the face!?"

As Rhyse got louder, Clint could feel the nervousness of the townspeople around him. With that last exclamation, some of the women in the crowd actually screamed as Rhyse pulled a chunk from his face and threw it at them. Clint could see what was happening and he knew he had only a few seconds to try and turn it around.

"He's just a man!" Clint shouted over the growing commotion. "He's a man made up to scare you people into doing what he says!" Looking up at the two other riders who were still on their mounts, Clint wondered why they hadn't done anything.

At the height of the panic he'd started, Rhyse pushed Clint with a forceful shove to his shoulders and stared at him through wild eyes. "Because of you, I'm gonna make this whole damn town an example. People got to learn not to stand in the way of death."

Clint saw Rhyse's hand move toward his gun and then reached for his own pistol, only to find an empty holster where his weapon should have been. Clint spun on the balls of his feet in search of his gun and saw it clutched in the hands of one of the townspeople who'd brought their shotguns to the saloon, supposedly to help get rid of Mason Rhyse.

"Give me my gun!" Clint shouted, even though the loudest

of the panicked locals had already fled. But he was incensed, both at the fact that someone would take his gun, and at the fact that he'd been so intent on Rhyse that he'd let it happen. If he died here today he deserved it.

The tall, gaunt man in the simple clothes took a few quick steps back while shaking his head. "Can't do it. Can't let the whole town be cursed in the name of one man who ain't even one of us."

Before Clint could say anything else, he felt a cold, iron grip on his left arm. Spinning around to face the one who'd grabbed him, Clint locked stares with Rhyse, who wore a wide, crazy smile made up of cracked lips and crooked teeth.

"They're smarter than you gave 'em credit for," Rhyse taunted as he slowly pulled his pistol free of its leather.

Clint easily tore free of Rhyse's hand by twisting his upper body around and drawing his hand in close to his chest. Like an uncoiling spring, he twisted his body back in the opposite direction and sent the back of his fist slamming into Rhyse's face. When the man went down in a mess of bony limbs and dirty braids, the other two riders finally started lowering themselves from their saddles.

Clint wanted to get his gun and take Monique to safety, but he knew he'd only be able to do one of those things before the other two riders started opening fire. The choice took a split second to make and within moments, Clint was barreling toward Monique, sweeping her into his arms and carrying her across the street to a small alley away from the saloon.

Gunshots cracked through the night, sending lead whipping in Clint's direction. The demonic sound of Rhyse howling wildly made him wonder if the man wasn't part demon after all.

EIGHTEEN

Most of the shots fired at them went wild, but still were enough to add speed to Clint and Monique's flight through the back-streets of Jespin. The sound of excited horses and Rhyse's barbaric screaming started to fade as they wound their way through the alleys and came out on the other side of town. Finally, Clint leaned back against the wall of a dry goods store to catch his breath.

"What the hell were you thinking back there?" Monique asked. She was too worked up to sit down, even though her breath came in ragged gasps. "Was all of that part of your great plan?"

"Well, not quite all of it," Clint said with a nervous laugh. "I thought that everyone else could see that Rhyse was obviously made up to look scary and that he could be hurt just like anyone else. It's plain to see that he's not a ghost, Monique."

"I know that, but why stir up so much commotion when Rhyse had you outnumbered three to one?"

Now Clint could feel his own anger bubbling to the surface. "Wait a second. We had him outnumbered! That is, unless I was imagining all those men standing next to me with shotguns in their hands. I thought they were there to back my play. Hell, they didn't have to do much besides look like they meant business. If Rhyse thought for a second that half of those men would fire on him, he would have turned tail and ran. It wasn't until he knew he had those people in his back pocket before everything turned bad."

Sighing, Monique put her head in her hands and ran her fingers over her scalp. The beads in her hair clinked together and her eyes were shut tight. "Clint, those people were ready to stand with you, but they just . . ."

"They got scared," he said, admitting it more to himself than to Monique. "My mistake was in thinking that they would want to do something about their fears. I thought they'd want to save their town. Isn't that why they came out there with me in the first place?"

Monique didn't quite know what to say. So instead of saying anything, she opened her eyes and straightened up until she was standing with her fists clenched. "I can still help you," she said. "And no matter what you think, these people here can help you just as much."

"After what happened back there," he said, shaking his head, "I can do without those people's brand of help."

The sounds of approaching hooves came around a corner and started coming down the street. Clint pushed Monique further into the shadows and took a peek around the edge of the building. He saw one of the big riders, a dark-skinned man wearing a string tie over a messy white shirt, who slowed his horse's pace and scanned the area as though he knew someone was hiding nearby.

Clint tensed in preparation to leap out after the horse moved past the alley, but was stopped by Monique's hands on his shoulders. The black man rode past, glancing into the shadows, but was unable to make out the figures huddled behind an empty crate. Seeing the back of the horse move past, Clint tried to move again, but quickly realized that Monique would force him to drag her behind him.

"I know a better way," she said once the horse was gone and Clint wheeled around for an explanation.

He allowed himself to be led down the alley until they came out on the other side. Looking around the building and down the street, Clint saw the rider had already passed and was turning to look in another part of town. When the coast was clear, Monique hurried across the street and ran up a short flight of stairs leading to a building that looked even more dead than Rhyse.

Monique tapped quickly on the door and just when Clint was starting to feel exposed in the open space, the door was tugged open and they rushed inside.

Clint found himself in what appeared to be a carpenter's workshop. The entire back wall was taken up by a huge wooden bench that came up a little higher than waist level. On it were tools of all kinds including saws, hammers, cups of nails and a worn metal lathe. Sawdust crunched beneath their feet as Clint and Monique moved away from the windows, which were hidden behind drawn curtains.

Once his eyes had adjusted to the thick blackness inside the dark room, Clint could make out four other figures huddling around Monique. The group stood around a pile of stacked lumber and even without the benefit of a lantern, Clint could see the fear in their eyes.

"We're safe here," Monique said. "These people talked to me earlier today when you were out scouting the town. After what you were saying, I think you'd have a lot in common with Mister O'Rielly."

At that point, a man roughly the same height as Clint stepped out of the group and extended his hand. His grip was strong and rough, obviously the hand of someone used to hard work. The man's face was round and covered with a thick beard. A mop of tangled hair fell down over his ears and eyes like an old mutt's.

"You're Mister Adams?" the man asked.

"That's right."

"I appreciate what you tried to do out there tonight. If I'd been closer to the action, I would have tried to help you, but I try to keep that bastard Rhyse out of my sight whenever I can."

"What are we here for?" Clint asked Monique.

"He knows what Rhyse wants and who," she answered.

"I already have a good idea what he wants," Clint said as he pulled the curtains aside just enough for him to glance outside. "What we need now is to get moving."

"I agree," O'Rielly said. The carpenter walked across the workshop and turned the knob on a lantern hanging from a hook on a post. He then carried the dim light over to a bench situated in the corner of the room and set the lantern on top of it.

Pressing his shoulder to the bench, O'Rielly shoved aside the heavy mass of wood with a labored grunt. The bench moved along the wall no more than a few inches and when Clint got closer, he saw a set of old grooves that had been gouged into the floor from all the other times that bench had been pushed aside.

O'Rielly squatted down and reached into a shallow hole beneath the bench, pulling out a large, oval-shaped bundle wrapped in blackened burlap. "Been savin' this for the right time," he said as he pulled away the covering to reveal a double-barreled shotgun that had been sawed off to less than half its original length. Nodding toward the hole beneath the bench, he added, "Needed to keep it away from the little ones."

Clint looked over to the group huddled in the shadows. Besides Monique, there was another woman, her pale skin catching what little light was available, and two small children who couldn't have been more than a few years old.

"I tried tellin' folks around here that Rhyse weren't nothin' but a man with a gun, but nobody wants to believe me," O'Rielly said solemnly. "I told Miss Monique last time she was here about my baby's earache that Rhyse would be comin' back to claim James Zeller's boy next."

Clint took the sawed-off shotgun and checked to make sure it was loaded. Both chambers were ready to go. "Why would he want this Zeller's son?"

"Cause Rhyse came ridin' out there a lot recently. He's a thief and he's been watching the Zeller's place like a bank robber watches the next place he's fixin' to hit. People been talkin' a lot lately about seeing them ghost riders around Zeller's property. Rhyse ain't stupid, so I'm sure he's been seen and figures on getting a hostage to make the whole job go smoother."

Smiling, Clint asked, "Have you always been a carpenter, O'Rielly?"

The other man laughed. "Hell no. Used to be a sheriff in Baton Rouge 'fore I got shot in the leg. My missus talked me into settling down and raising a family." He tapped his temple and gave a quick wink. "Still got the eye, though."

"That you do, my friend." Clint snapped the shotgun closed with a flick of his wrist. "Is the Zeller's place one of those big houses on the edge of town?"

"Sure enough. Got its own little dock on the river and a patch of land besides."

"I've seen it. There's a lot of armed men waiting for trouble out there."

"That's why Rhyse came into town tonight. That Zeller boy, Aubrey, is here gettin' drunk just like he does every night and takin' him here is a whole lot easier than breakin' through those men you saw."

"The more I hear, the less demonic this Rhyse becomes," Clint said. "I've looked into his eyes and he's nothing more than an outlaw with a gimmick."

O'Rielly slapped him on the shoulder and boomed, "Voodoo my ass! No offense, meant," he added while turning toward Monique.

From outside, the sound of gunfire could be heard echoing from the next street over. Clint didn't need to look out the window to know who was pulling those triggers. "Thank you very much for the help," Clint said to O'Rielly as the carpenter pressed four more shotgun shells into his palm. Turning toward Monique, he began to talk, but was interrupted.

"Don't try to talk me out of it, Clint," she said in a rush. "I'm coming with you."

"I was just going to ask if you would come with me."

Her eyes registered Monique's surprise. "Really?"

"I need you. Rhyse may be trying to fool us, but those men with him are believers. If reason couldn't work on the locals, I won't even try it on the converted, so you need to help me." They hurried out the back door of the workshop and emerged in another, much narrower alley. "Did your mother ever teach you how to do an exorcism?"

NINETEEN

The night had become unnaturally quiet. Even the normal blanket of sounds ranging from the chirping of insects to the croak of frogs seemed to have been sucked from the very air that had carried it in from the nearby river. As for the people living in the town of Jespin, it was as though they, too, had been hidden away by the ghostly figures patrolling the streets.

Clint had one hand around Monique's wrist and gripped the blunted shotgun in the other. Their footsteps were like little explosions in the silence and every step they took seemed as though it would surely bring their pursuers down upon them.

At first, Clint thought Rhyse would hunt him down as a matter of pride after being humiliated in front of his men. If things had gone the way they were supposed to, Rhyse would have been worked up enough to make a mistake that would have allowed him to be captured by Clint and the makeshift posse he'd formed. But things hadn't gone right.

Not at all.

The longer Clint and Monique ran, however, the more convinced they became that they were the ones doing the chasing.

"These tracks lead out of town," Clint said after they'd come to a stop outside a livery.

"Isn't Rhyse looking for us anymore?" Monique asked.

"He was, but not for long. I'd say for the last half hour or so Rhyse has just been circling the town to gather up his men and head them out."

"Toward the Zeller house?"

"Looks like it." Taking a moment to get his bearings, Clint figured that they were less than half a mile away from the banks of the Mississippi. "The house with all the guards is straight ahead and that's where Rhyse wants to go. He probably wanted to keep on schedule."

"Why would he let you go so easily?"

"Because that would be the smart thing to do, Monique. Outlaws are easier to catch when they're running around on some spur of the moment decision. Rhyse keeps to his plan and keeps in control. Now we've just got to catch up to him."

Heading straight back to the saloon was risky, but it was also the ultimate way to test Clint's theory. Just as he'd thought, none of the riders showed up before Clint was climbing up onto Eclipse's saddle.

"If we head out now, we might catch them," Clint said as he helped Monique up onto the stallion.

The Darley Arabian took off like he'd been shot from a cannon. The streets sped beneath them, soon to be replaced by trees that whipped over their heads. Before they knew it, they could see the first hint of lights from the Zeller estate in the distance. Clint drew Eclipse to a halt before breaking cover and dropped to the ground.

When he heard the footsteps coming from the direction of the small wooden dock, Clint brought up his shotgun and spun to face whoever was approaching. At first, all he saw was the figure of a man walking toward him. A ghostly face wearing a calm curious expression hung as if suspended in the air. Clint recognized the face as soon as he heard the figure speak.

"Is that you, Clint?" Joseph Terray asked as he stepped closer.

Without lowering the gun, Clint took a closer look until he was absolutely sure of what he saw. "How you feeling, Joseph? From what I hear, you're not doing too well."

"What are you doing out here?" Then Joseph saw the woman on Clint's horse and his eyes grew wide. "Miss Monique?"

Without missing a beat, Clint swung the shotgun around to catch Joseph on the back of the neck. The man dropped to the ground in an unconscious heap, letting a pistol fall from his grasp. After dragging him into the cover of the surrounding trees, Clint took what weapons he could find from Joseph's pockets. The pistol he found would more than likely blow up in his hand if he tried to fire it. He discarded it.

"Why'd you do that?" Monique asked in an urgent whisper.

"Look at him." Clint pointed to Terray's face, which was covered with the pale mixture of muddy paste that had marked Rhyse and his men. "He's with Rhyse now. I couldn't take the chance of letting him tell the others where we were."

Monique stared down at the other man and hopped out of the saddle. Crouching next to Joseph, she ran her finger over his cheeks and felt the grayish substance covering his skin. Then, she pressed her fingers to the side of his neck. "He's got a pulse," she said as though convincing herself of the fact.

Clint removed a length of rope that was hanging from Eclipse's saddle. Using it to tie up Joseph's arms and legs, he made sure the other man wouldn't be able to do much of anything when he came around. He was about to head toward the estate when the sound of heavy hoofbeats seemed to come at him from every direction.

The shotgun was back in his hand and ready to fire by the time Rhyse's horse emerged from the trees. The priest's collar showed up brighter than anything else in the darkness, hovering high in the air atop a dark gray mare. A few more steps and the horse carried Rhyse close enough for Clint to see the smug, self-satisfied expression on his face.

"You may not believe in the spirits in these here swamps," Rhyse said as he brought his horse to a stop next to Eclipse. "But they been tellin' me an awful lot about you. They told me that if I just sat and waited before going into that den of rich sinners over there, that you would come to me. And jus' look . . ."

The other heavy steps belonged to the horses of Rhyse's two remaining men. When Clint looked toward them, he saw the black rider with the string tie coming up behind Eclipse and could hear another as it drew to a stop behind him.

"You come to me jus' like they said."

If he'd had his pistol, Clint figured he might have stood a chance against the three riders. As it was, even if he'd been fast enough to get the drop on all of them, the shotgun in his hands only held two rounds. Besides, a shot in Rhyse's direction would more than likely have hit Eclipse as well as Monique.

Unlike before, both men he could see had pulled their guns and were aiming them at Clint. And just to make sure that he knew about it, the man behind him snapped back the hammer of his pistol, which echoed coldly in Clint's ears.

Clint opened his hand and let the shotgun drop to the ground at his feet. A tall man wearing a ratty black coat stepped from behind him and reached down for the fallen weapon. Just as he was about to make a move, Clint felt the cold unforgiving steel of another gun barrel being jammed into his spine. Every muscle ached to move and Clint had to struggle to keep from lashing out at the closest man.

"I think I'll leave this place for now," Rhyse said. "I can always come back later to rob them rich folks. Their money will still be there. I'm sure. Besides, you both make a better prize than any amount of cash."

Clint watched as the black rider climbed down from his horse and grabbed hold of Monique by the back of her collar. Even as he took her down from Eclipse's back, he handled her with a certain respect and gentleness. Tying her hands together, he made sure that the ropes didn't chew too deeply into her skin.

Rhyse looked on like a proud father. "Especially that witch," he said while staring at Monique. "She gonna be the feather in my cap." Then he turned back toward Clint to say, "But don't feel bad, now. I'm sure I can make you see the error of your ways. In fact, I'll even drink on it."

The long coat that was wrapped around Rhyse's body seemed to peel open of its own accord. His black-gloved hands went to one of the inner pockets to pull out a dented copper flask. Rhyse twisted the top open and waved it under his nose before tossing it down to the man who'd just finished tying Clint's arms together. "That's the good stuff. Eddie, make sure he gets a drink."

The story Kim Terray had told him raced through Clint's mind as the flask drew closer to his mouth. He pictured the patch of flattened weeds and the bullet holes in the ground behind Joseph's home. All the stories he'd heard about Mason Rhyse and all the outlandish voodoo tales came rushing back to him. Suddenly, they didn't seem so silly anymore.

Clint pressed his mouth shut as the warm metal was pushed against it. Some of the whiskey splashed onto his face and landed on his bottom lip, making the skin tingle and go numb with the touch of potent whiskey. But there was something else there, too. It was something that, even though he hadn't let a drop of the stuff go down his throat, still made him feel a little shaky and weak in the knees.

Rhyse's voice sounded to Clint as though it was muddier than the waters of the nearby river. "Go on," it said. "Give 'im his drink."

A fist came from out of nowhere and slammed Clint across the jaw. When his lips parted, a dirty finger jammed in between them, soon to be followed by a bitter flood of alcohol that warmed his throat and sent him plummeting into a deep sleep.

TWENTY

Clint dreamed of falling. His body bounced off the sides of an endless canyon before tumbling once more into the abyss. Every once in a while, he could hear a voice calling his name or that of somebody else, but for the most part, there was nothing.

When the sounds became a constant babbling rush, he could smell the damp odor of the swamp. It filled his nose and clung to the back of his mouth like a foul jelly. His sense of taste came back just in time for him to regret it and when the bile rose up from his stomach in reaction to the mixture of mold and soil, Clint's muscles twitched and jumped beneath his skin.

He opened his eyes, only to clamp them shut immediately. Something was pressing against his face that had stung his eyeballs with an intense scratching. Still feeling as though he was tumbling downward, Clint realized that he'd been lying facedown at an angle that pressed his nose into the bayou floor.

Struggling to get to his feet, Clint instantly discovered that he could barely move. The ropes were no longer around his wrists or ankles, but there was something pressing down on his entire body like a blanket of lead holding him in place. With a concentrated push, he used all the strength he had. Digging his fingers and toes into the ground, Clint forced his body upward . . . and moved about two inches.

The effort wore on his system and at that point he realized that whatever had been in that whiskey was still flowing through his blood. Although weakened over time, the potent formula was still enough to make every movement a straining effort. Clint allowed himself to relax for a moment and concentrated on figuring out how long he'd been Rhyse's prisoner.

Without being able to see any trace of the outside world or even a glimpse of the sky, any guess on whether it was day or night would have been nothing more than a fifty-fifty shot. He did not know that he was trapped in what had to be some kind of cellar in the middle of the swamp. Either that or . . .

Suddenly, Clint knew why his nose and mouth were filled with putrid soil and what it was that weighed down on his entire back. He wasn't in a cellar, although he knew for a fact he was underground.

Rhyse had buried him alive!

When that realization hit, Clint found more energy inside of him than he ever thought possible.

The next time he pushed himself, he swore he could feel something above him beginning to budge. It was only then that he knew he was running on pure instinct when he was figuring which way was up. As far as he knew, he might have been trying to push himself deeper into the loose ground and wouldn't find out his mistake until he'd gone too far to come back up again.

At that point, there would be nothing left to breathe but dirt and the last thing he would touch on this earth would be the slimy grit beneath his fingernails. As he was thinking this, Clint was still busy pushing his way through the ground like some kind of giant earthworm. If nothing else, he was working his body free so that he could move just a little bit more every time he pushed. Finally, he could raise up as high as if he was doing a push-up and when he dropped back down again, he could tell by the way the earth pressed down on him that he was indeed facing down.

The next time he pushed up, Clint could start to see the slightest hint of light cracking in to tease his peripheral vision. If he wasn't mistaken, he could also hear muffled voices coming from the surface. One of those voices belonged to Rhyse and the other was Monique's. She was crying.

With one last shove, Clint strained all the muscles in his

arms and chest until they felt like they were about to snap off his bones. Wriggling like an eel, he managed to roll over onto his back, reach up through the dirt to grab a hold of . . . empty air.

He was out.

Clint pressed his palms against the ground and used his grip to hoist himself into the open. When he was almost there, he sat up and took in a deep lungful of the moist, bayou air. At that moment, the bog smelled sweet as a field of wildflowers and the sky looked like heaven itself.

The next thing to enter his field of vision was the face of Mason Rhyse.

"Welcome back," Rhyse said while pulling Clint the rest of the way from the hole in which he'd been planted. "Join me now, or I'll plant you back into that grave of yours."

Without even hesitating, Clint took the hand Rhyse offered and got to his feet.

TWENTY-ONE

Clint spent the better part of the day listening to Rhyse preach to him about pulling him out of his own grave and bringing him back from the jaws of death. For the most part, Clint heard nothing but an endless stream of babble coming from the mud-covered man that was supposed to make him feel like he owed Rhyse his soul.

It didn't work.

Instead, Clint used that time to get his strength back and try to get the taste of the swamp out of his mouth. Whenever Rhyse looked to him for some kind of pledge of loyalty or a nod of agreement, Clint gladly gave it to him. The longer Rhyse could be stalled, the stronger Clint could become before making his break for it.

Besides realizing that Rhyse was completely insane, Clint also spent that day watching the others. With the preacher's voice droning on and on, Clint focused in on everyone else. Otherwise, the constant barrage of words might have been enough to start swinging his thoughts in the wrong direction.

The one called Lovario and his friend Stokes seemed to buy in to the preacher's stories. Although they didn't look happy to be there, the nods and pledges they gave were genuine. They honestly felt that they owed Rhyse their lives, instead of hating him for burying them in a hole after drugging them senseless.

Joseph sat by himself for the most part, tending to Monique when she needed water or food. While he seemed to believe what Rhyse was saying, there also seemed to be a spark of doubt in the way he avoided Rhyse's eyes and stayed well away from the other two men.

Monique was holding up rather well considering all that had happened. She seemed to perk up especially when Clint would look her way and give her a wink to let her know he was alright. Her face was dirty and her hair was matted down with sweat and mud. Even though she was tied at the wrists and ankles, she kept her head held high.

Judging by the position of the sun and its movement, Clint figured he'd been awake for about twelve hours. Only then did Rhyse start letting up on his rambling voodoo speech. Honestly, Clint would have been hard-pressed to say what the preacher had been talking about all this time since he'd been doing his best to ignore him. What he did know was that it was almost time to move.

". . . and believe me, I will ask for your sacrifice," Rhyse said in a voice that was becoming a hoarse croak. "You've joined us at the right time, my friend. For when we roll through these towns, we will be like the thunder and they will fall at our feet."

Just to make things easier, Clint nodded and got to his feet. He exaggerated how weak his legs were, hoping he wasn't overdoing the effect. "I . . . I need some water," he said.

Rhyse waved his hands toward a pile of packs and canteens set up near an old fallen log. "Sure thing. Help yourself."

Clint walked across the small camp that had been set up in a large clearing on relatively solid ground. He didn't even need his eyes open to know they were in the bayou. The stench of mold, rotting wood and putrid water permeated every pore in his skin and had long ago soaked into his clothes. At the edge of the clearing, close to a pool of standing water that was thick with lizards and green fungus, was a small campfire that was currently nothing but a pile of blackened sticks. Lovario and Stokes sat near the water, swatting at mosquitoes the size of crickets.

Monique was leaning against a hollow log. The riders had stacked all their packs and supplies there and didn't seem to mind Monique being so close to it since, with her hands and feet tied securely, she was little more than just another one of their possessions. She watched him approach with concern in her eyes and was about to say something before Clint stopped her with a swift wave of his hand.

Staggering over to the canteens, he looked quickly over his shoulder to make sure that Rhyse was busy with his men. "How long have we been here?" he asked quietly.

"About a day and a half. I thought you were dead when they buried you in that hole." Looking over her shoulder, Monique glanced behind the log to a patch of disturbed ground roughly the size and shape of a casket. "You came out of there a few minutes later and then passed out until this morning."

Seeing the hole that Rhyse had dug for him, Clint felt a fire burning deep in his gut. It must have shown on his face because Monique put her hands delicately on Clint's while softly stroking his skin.

"I wish I could have stopped them," she said soothingly. "But he was waiting for you. They knew you'd come out."

"Yeah. I'll bet they did," Clint said as he reached down for one of the canteens. "Is this water ok?"

"Yes. I've been drinking from it all day and it's not drugged."

Taking a swig of the cold water, Clint savored the feel of it washing down his throat, cleaning him as it went along. "We're getting out of here tonight," he said. "And we're taking Joseph with us."

At first, Monique was excited. But just as quickly as it came, the emotion left her. "But, he's one of them now. I can see it in his eyes. He'll try to stop us."

"That's why we need to get him alone and away from these others. You can help me break him out of this." Clint took another deep drink and checked Rhyse. The preacher was looking over to him occasionally, but only for a glance. Then Clint looked over to Joseph. The short, stocky man was sitting along on the edge of the camp, intently watching him and Monique.

"He's not a killer," Clint whispered while keeping his eyes on Joseph. "He's been talked into something that he doesn't even want to accept. He shouldn't be here following Rhyse around like he's some kind of god."

"And what about them?" Monique asked, nodding toward Lovario and Stokes. "They deserve to be here?"

"I've got a plan, Monique. We'll help the others too, but

first we need to turn one of them away from Rhyse and Joseph's our best chance."

"What's that witch tellin' you?" Rhyse shouted while standing and walking over to where Clint was crouched. "You don't listen to her. Her magic is twisted and unclean. She wants us dead. All of us."

Without saying a word, Clint stood, dropped the canteen to the ground and stared at Monique with the look that was filled with all the hate Rhyse had been hoping to inspire. Rhyse put a hand on his shoulder and pulled him toward the fire that was being started near the water.

"Come, my friend. I know the grave is a cold place, so we're starting a fire for you. We've got to go over our plans. Why don't you go and bring Joseph with you?"

Clint nodded and walked over to where Joseph was sitting. Putting his back to Rhyse and the other men, Clint crouched down to Joseph's level. "You remember me, buddy?" he whispered. "You told me to stop by whenever I was coming through the area."

Squinting, Joseph turned his head like a puzzled dog. "Clint Adams? Is that really you?"

"Sure is. All I wanted was some of Kim's gumbo and look what happens."

"But, if you're here . . . then."

"Didn't you see me earlier?"

Joseph rubbed his eyes and took a deep breath. "It's been a while, Clint. Jesus, even last week seems like years ago to me. It's all such a blur."

"Don't worry about that. We'll talk later. Right now, we've got to sit in on another one of the crazy man's speeches."

"But Rhyse isn't crazy," Joseph said as though he was reciting lines from a script. "He saved me. Saved us all."

Clint was about to say something else to the man, but Rhyse was calling for them to come over by the water. Besides that, it was obvious that Joseph wasn't as open to suggestion as he normally would be. Not from Clint, anyway.

All he had to do, Clint knew, was to get Joseph to listen to him the way he listened to Rhyse. And that, unfortunately, might not be too easy. It wasn't every day that Clint had to compete with a man's personal savior for attention.

In a strange kind of way, Clint had to give Rhyse credit. The preacher was good at what he did. Unfortunately for Rhyse, so was Clint.

TWENTY-TWO

One of the biggest faults a criminal could have was to possess more guts than brains. Even though Rhyse had cooked up a fairly hokey scheme in Clint's opinion, it seemed to be working well enough. As much as he hated to admit it, Clint realized that everyone except for Mr. O'Rielly was taken in by the voodoo displays.

But it was that old fault that served as Rhyse's curse. Even though there were probably double the guards and triple the guns around Zeller's estate, Rhyse was still planning on going back there when the night was at its darkest.

"Why?" Clint asked during the discussion around a fire that had just been started. "Why go back there?"

As the sun appeared to dip into the furthest reaches of the swamp to get snuffed out like a giant candle, the flame's light danced across the men's faces to create an eerie display of shadow. The quiet raiders were dipping their fingers into a small wooden bowl and applying a rank mixture to their skin. With every stroke of their hand, the men looked more like the demons they were supposed to be.

"We're going back there for the same reason as before," Rhyse explained.

Lovario grunted as his fingertips slid over his skin. The muddy paste glowed with a pale luminescence in the firelight. "I used to work for that family when I was a living man. They ain't nothin' but a greedy bunch of cheats who'll do anything

90

that'll put a dollar in their pockets." Turning to face Clint, the tall man looked fresh from the grave with clots of dirt clinging to his mustache. "And they'll do anything for their son."

Suddenly, Rhyse's hand came flashing over the little fire to smack Lovario across the face with enough force to send him toppling over sideways. The preacher's eyes seemed to catch the flames. He'd applied so much of the paste to his skin that it fused the priest's collar to his neck. With the sudden movement, the mud had cracked in places, making it look as though his skull was splitting apart.

"That's enough of that talk!" Rhyse shouted. "All he needs to know is what I tell 'im. Nothing more."

Clint watched the preacher calm himself down and felt a nudge on his arm. It was Stokes, prodding him with the edge of the little wooden bowl. Taking the container in his hand, Clint dipped his fingers in the paste and sniffed at the vile concoction. "Why do we need this?" he asked.

"Same reason the Injuns need their war paint," Rhyse explained. "It shows the spirits whose side we're on, so that when we call down their judgment, we're the only ones left standin'."

It took all Clint had to keep his expression from registering his true feelings. Putting on his best poker face, Clint smeared some of the stuff on and tried not to breathe in through his nose. "What am I supposed to do when we get to Zeller's?"

Rhyse stared at Clint for the better part of a minute. The tension would have been uncomfortable if not for the fact that everyone else seemed used to such heavy silences. "You do what I tell ya," he finally said. "And nothin' more."

After that, the camp was silent. Even Monique watched the men get ready without saying a word. When Clint looked over to her, she held her head high and nodded solemnly to let him know she was fine. As much as he wanted to go over and comfort her or even make a break for the surrounding marsh, Clint held himself back and finished getting ready for the night's raid.

Like a well-oiled machine, Rhyse and his men set about taking down the camp. Joseph busied himself with gathering up the packs and headed off into the trees. Clint started to follow, but froze when he heard Rhyse calling for him.

"You there," the preacher said since he still didn't know

Clint's name. "Take this." In the preacher's hand was O'Rielly's sawed-off shotgun. "You'll get your bullets if you need them, but we rarely need to pull our weapons."

"What if someone shoots at me?"

"They can't kill what's already dead."

Clint couldn't think of a way to argue with the man's logic without giving away the fact that he wasn't buying into it. Out of reflex, he opened the breach of the shotgun and looked inside. Empty. At least Rhyse didn't lie about everything.

"Joseph," Rhyse shouted. "Take her and see that she doesn't make any noise. At least, not until we get close enough for her screams to be heard."

The group walked through the bayou, with Lovario in the lead and Rhyse behind, followed by Clint and Stokes with Joseph and Monique bringing up the rear. She'd been untied to make travel easier. As they sloshed their way through the dark bog, the marching order switched several times, but only to let Stokes slip into the rear position so he could keep a better eye on the rest.

Clint followed along, watching the men as they stepped over sleeping reptiles and sunk knee-deep in hot, fetid waters. The cicadas chirped in a single grating voice that sounded like the very pulse of the bayou itself. The rhythm rose and fell, rose and fell, faster and faster before suddenly dying off, only to start again.

And like the cicadas, Rhyse started his sermons again as well. He preached his connection to the dead and emphasized how lucky his men were to be saved from their horrible fates. At one point, he passed around his flask. Clint noticed that Rhyse only put the copper container to his lips but didn't drink before handing it back. Going through the same motions as Rhyse, Clint held his breath and pretended to drink, knowing full well that Rhyse would start making a lot of sense if he swallowed any of whatever drug the preacher had used to spike that whiskey.

Turning with the flask in hand, Clint saw Joseph reaching out to take a drink. That's when Clint knew that now was the time to move.

TWENTY-THREE

Clint held the flask in his hand, stretching back as though he was about to hand it over to Joseph. As Joseph walked up closer to him, Clint turned and glanced over to Monique. She was ready.

Moving so that he was facing the back of the line, Clint held the flask in both hands while fidgeting with the metal cap attached to the neck. He appeared to be having trouble with something, but didn't say a word until he figured Rhyse and Lovario had gone a little ways up the path.

"Here you go," Clint said once Joseph had stopped and Stokes was drawing closer. "Rhyse wanted you to have this." Suddenly, Clint's arm struck outward to slam the flask along the side of Stokes's head. The impact made a dull thud which sounded like a mallet striking against a moss-covered rock.

Clint didn't wait for the tall black man to react. Instead, he sent his fist crashing downward to connect with Joseph's wrist. The quick, sharp pain of the blow caused Joseph to let go of Monique and as soon as she was free, she jumped off the trail and into the surrounding foliage.

Joseph looked confused, but rather than debate with him, Clint reached for the other man's holster and removed Joseph's gun. In a flash, Clint had the old pistol in hand and was pointing at its owner. It was the same gun he'd taken from Joseph before and still wasn't sure it would fire properly.

"Go with Monique," Clint said quickly and quietly.

Before Joseph could think of anything better to do, Monique was dragging him by the arm and into the surrounding brush. Clint looked further up the path to see that Rhyse and Lovario had already turned around a large tree whose trunk was as big around as both their bodies combined. Not wanting to press his luck, Clint stepped over to Stokes and reached out for that man's gun.

He was inches away from the holster before a strong hand clamped around Clint's wrist. Clint looked up into Stokes's face to see the black man shaking his head to clear out the fog that the canteen had created when it bounced off his skull. Clint was about to put the man down with a blow from the butt of Joseph's revolver, but Stokes surprised him by lashing out with a fast right hook.

Stokes's fist was as big around as a small grapefruit and when it caught Clint on the jaw, it forced bright dancing stars in front of his eyes. Reeling back from the impact, Clint instinctually ducked as the bigger man's other arm came swinging around for a follow-up. The lunging punch sounded like a piece of timber being swung over Clint's head and would have been enough to knock him into tomorrow if it had connected.

Further up the path, Clint could hear the sounds of voices calling Stokes's name. He knew he had to get away now or the escape would be over before it started. Just as Stokes was winding up for another punch, Clint sent a sharp jab into his stomach, which doubled Stokes over just in time for Clint to bring his knee up into the man's jaw.

Stokes reeled back with blood streaming from his mouth as Rhyse came running back to see what had happened. Clint was off the path and into the woods before he realized he'd left Stokes's gun in its holster. It was too late to turn back, so Clint kept running forward until he caught up with Monique and Joseph.

Still clutching Joseph's gun, Clint swung it toward the other man and growled, "Hand over the shells to my shotgun."

Mason Rhyse had his hands gripped tightly around Lovario's arm. When he'd heard the commotion behind him, he didn't even have to look to know it was being caused by the newest addition to his clergy. Lovario had wanted to go charging off to see what had happened, but Rhyse kept him in place.

"You don't go running into the inferno," Rhyse said while pulling his gun from under his long black coat. He tilted his head and closed his eyes.

Lovario watched his leader and thought the smaller man was hearing voices being whispered by spirits.

"They tryin' to escape," Rhyse stated simply. "Stick to the side of the path and look out when you turn that corner." Then he shoved Lovario down the path and followed closely after him.

They made it just in time to see Stokes reeling back in pain and Clint taking off into the bush.

"Get them!" Rhyse screamed. His voice came out of him like an angry ghost charging from the pits of hell and even Stokes pushed aside the pain to obey that command.

Joseph fumbled at the packs on his shoulders for a second before he came across a bundle cinched together with twine. Clint could hear the other two men walking slowly toward them as he took the bundle and untied the twine. Most of the shells fell to the ground at his feet, but Clint managed to grab two of them just as he caught the first sight of Stokes peeking at them from behind an overhanging veil of mossy green.

Monique was trying to say something while pointing a nervous finger toward the black man. Joseph started to make a move for Clint, but wasn't able to do anything before the shotgun was loaded. Clint snapped it shut with a quick motion and brought it up to cover Stokes.

The towering black man moved through the weeds like a snake, his feet automatically adjusting to the loose ground squishing beneath him. Times like these made Stokes feel the strength he'd brought back from the grave and when he poked his head through a hanging curtain of vines to find himself looking down the barrel of a shotgun, it was that speed that kept his head on his shoulders.

The first thing Clint saw was the glint of metal flashing in Stokes's hand and then he pulled his trigger. Everything in front of him was clouded in smoke. Thunder from the shotgun blared in his ears. Not wanting to wait and see what he'd hit, Clint turned and grabbed hold of the front of Joseph's coat

and pulled him deeper into the swamp. Monique had already
started running to keep up with Clint.

Heat from the blast singed his hair and the explosion deafened
him, but Stokes had ducked down fast enough to let the hail-
storm of lead pass over him and nearly cut an old tree in half.
    "Go around to cut them off," Rhyse commanded. But Stokes
wasn't responding. He was moving, but all he could do was
shake his head and press his hands over his ears. Turning to
Lovario, he commanded, "Let them get ahead of us and then
track them down. We'll come in from behind and trap them
in between."
    "What about the Zeller boy?" Lovario asked.
    "I can see through every last eye in this swamp and can feel
every foot that presses against this ground. We'll find those
traitors who deny my gift and then steal the rich man's son
before the dawn."

While they were running, Joseph easily twisted out of Clint's
grasp. They'd gone about fifty feet before Joseph stopped and
turned on them both. "Let me go! I gotta stay with Rhyse!"
    "I don't have time for this," Clint said. During his search
for the shotgun shells, Clint had tucked Joseph's gun into his
waistband. Now, he reached behind him, removed the pistol
and handed it over to Joseph. "Here you go," Clint said.
"Rhyse cares so much for you. He takes care of you. Why
don't you shoot me and go back to him?"
    The expression on Joseph's face switched back and forth
between confusion and anger. He gripped the gun unsteadily
at first, but then seemed to find a resolve within himself and
put the tip of the barrel against Clint's chest.
    "Go ahead and do it, Joseph. Kill me in the name of the
great Mason Rhyse."
    Joseph squinted as though he was trying to look at the sun.
Then, while letting a shaky breath escape from his throat, he
grit his teeth . . . and pulled the trigger.
    Click
    When the hammer fell onto the empty chamber, Monique
jumped higher than anyone else. Joseph shook his head slowly
and Clint reached forward to push the pistol away from him.

"That's how Rhyse protects you," Clint said. "If there was any trouble at Zeller's house or anywhere else along the way, you would have been shot down without a chance to fight back."

When Joseph opened his eyes again, he seemed to feel more like the man he was than the dead soul he'd been turned in to. "Clint? Why did I try to kill you?"

Looking for any sign of their pursuers, Clint spotted some movement coming their way. "Because Rhyse is a manipulating bastard who gets you to believe he controls your every move."

"How 'bout we discuss this later?" Monique said as she eagerly headed away from the approaching men.

Clint stood for a second to study the mixed emotions on Joseph's face. It was hard for him to imagine what the other man could have been thinking, but he knew he saw the sting of shame creeping through the other man.

"Let's go," Clint said. "You make your choice right now." And then Clint turned his back on him and headed off further into the swamps.

Joseph thought about going back to Rhyse, but then memories of everything else in his life came rushing back to him. His home, his friends, his work and most of all his beloved Kim. Rubbing his hands over his eyes, Joseph felt like his senses were finally coming back to him. After that, the choice was easy.

Quickly, he bent down to scoop up the fallen shotgun shells and then took off after Clint and Monique.

Rhyse helped Stokes to his feet, told him where Clint and the others were headed and sent him on his way. Then he went back to Lovario and pulled the gun from his holster. "These bullets I'm givin' to you," he said while filling empty chambers with live rounds, "are cursed. They'll send them they touch to a place deep within the belly of the demon."

Lovario never thought to question why his gun hadn't been loaded before. All he heard was the mystical chants of the scrawny man in the priest's collar. When he held that gun back in his hand, Lovario felt unstoppable.

And still, Rhyse preached on. "Zeller will pay to get his boy back. Then the next ones will pay just to keep us from darkening their door. After that, the fear will grow until it makes us rich enough to leave these swamps for good. Every town will pay, but those out there runnin' . . . they'll pay in blood."

TWENTY-FOUR

It took every bit of Clint's concentration to be able to tell one inch of the bayou from another. In the time it had taken for them to get Rhyse's men off their tails, every trace of the light in the sky had been leeched away by the night. Now, all was damp, dripping darkness. Water was always under their feet, the insects were always loudly chirping and there was always something biting at their heels.

Before long, Clint's eyes had adjusted to the inky blackness. His hand never broke contact with Monique's arm and Joseph had become a solid shadow leading the way. These weren't Joseph's swamps, but he knew how and where to step. It was all Clint could do just to keep up.

"Hold on for a second," Clint said. "We need to know where we're headed before we run too far in the wrong direction."

Even with his blood pumping like quicksilver through his veins and the mud seeping into his boots, Joseph was actually beginning to feel alive again. "I won't let you go in the wrong direction. I kept my eyes open when Rhyse led me through here an' I can get you back out."

Clint couldn't keep the short laugh from slipping out. "Well, I don't know about anyone else, but I can barely see my hand in front of my face."

Playfully slapping Clint on the back, Joseph said, "Good thing you ain't leadin' us then, eh?"

Monique didn't even pretend to join in on the men's nervous

laughter. "Maybe I'm the only one who remember the killers chasin' us? I think we need to—"

Her words stopped as if they'd been snuffed out like a candle. Drawing in her breath slowly and carefully, Monique gripped Clint's hand and pulled him closer to her. "Something just crawled over my feet," she whispered.

"It's the swamp," Clint said. "There's been something crawling on me since I got here." Looking to Joseph, Clint could barely make out the other man as he moved cautiously toward them.

Joseph reached around his back to pull out a blade that was too small to be considered a machete, but way too big to be just a knife. "She's right," he said. "There's somethin' here. Nobody move."

As much as Monique wanted to stay absolutely still, she couldn't keep the shakes from rattling her entire body. She could still feel what had touched her moments ago. It was no snake slithering over her toes or even a lizard scurrying around her ankles. What she'd felt was something else. Something stepped on her and brushed by her lower leg that felt tough and leathery. Even after it had passed, she could hear the creature's heavy breathing.

Clint was about to question her when he felt something as well. It was like a thick branch wrapped in bone. It was a tail and it damn near swept his feet out from under him.

"It's a gator," Joseph whispered. "Must've fed already since it didn't come right at us."

"Does that mean we're safe?" Monique asked hopefully.

"Not hardly. It jus' means that it'll take its time and circle us before taking us down."

Suddenly, the night seemed especially dark.

Thinking about which way the gator had crawled, Clint began to slowly walk in the opposite direction. His hand got a firm grip on Monique's elbow and led her in the same direction. His other hand held on to the shotgun, thumbing back the second hammer in preparation for the next time he felt the big reptile crawl by.

"OK, Joseph," Clint whispered. "This is your territory. What do we do here?"

From what could be seen in the murky shadows, Joseph was crouched down low, feeling the ground with his empty hand.

"We're right at the edge of a deep part in the water. Gators make their homes underneath. This one prob'ly takin' a fresh kill below to store for a while an' will come back for us then."

Suddenly, they all heard a deep splashing sound coming from directly in front of where they were standing. Clint could tell just by listening that whatever had broken the water was very large. When the sound faded, he began to move along what he guessed was the bank of the pond.

"Slowly," Joseph warned. "Move fast and it'll just be invitin' that thing back up here."

Monique spoke in a voice that was shaking on the verge of tears. "If that means we can run, I'm willing to take that chance."

Clint kept his steps even and slow, but moving steadily away. "Can these things run very fast, Joseph?"

"Yeah, but only in a straight line. It starts chasin', you'd better run in a zig-zag. That way, it got to slow down to make those turns."

"Great," Clint said sarcastically. "We can either wind up heading right back into Rhyse's arms or run zig-zag through a swamp in the dark from a hungry alligator. No offense, but your wife's cooking isn't worth this much trouble."

As their eyes adjusted to the dark, they could make out more of their surroundings. Mainly, they could see they were walking on a bank of reeds that looked like a field that had been flooded after a heavy rain. But the waters were still and appeared thick in the dim moonlight. There was movement out there, but only ripples. Behind them, the bayou became a dense maze of logs, mildew-encrusted trees and other patches of water that could have been puddles or deep enough to drown a man.

"Come on," Joseph whispered. "If we move now, we might just get out of here before that thing come back up for air."

Clint made sure that he had a firm hold on Monique's arm. Since he could just barely see where he was walking, he needed to know where she was at. Even with her heart pounding in her chest and nervous sweat beading on her forehead, Monique took Clint's lead as if they were on a dance floor. Her body moved like one of the lithe cats in her living room back home.

With his senses reaching out for any stray sound or movement around him, Clint could hear the faint noise of footsteps squishing in the trees back in the direction from which they'd come. Straining his ears for details, he could eventually hear twigs snapping and a single whispered word.

Clint let go of Monique so he could reach out and tap Joseph on the shoulder. The smaller man swiveled his head around and gave a few sharp nods to let Clint know that he'd heard the sounds too. As much as he wanted to put his trust in the man, Clint's survival sense told him to keep in mind how Joseph had spent his last few days. Just to be sure, Clint held the shotgun up at his waist level, ready to fire on Joseph if he decided that he was still on Rhyse's side.

They were still moving along the banks, heading slowly away from the water when the steps behind them began to quicken. Without turning around to try and see their pursuers, Clint and Monique started to hurry for the cover of the thick tangle of overhanging moss since Joseph had already taken refuge behind a thick tree trunk.

"I see them," came the voice of Willie Stokes from the edge of the pond. Heavy footsteps began to slosh toward Clint's back just as another voice hissed in the darkness.

"Watch it there." It was Lovario. "Get away from dat water!"

But it was too late. Suddenly, the waters erupted outward as though someone had dropped a stick of dynamite below the floating lily pads. Amid the loud crash of the breaking water, there was a deep rumble that was something between a gurgle and a growl. Putrid water sprayed up to douse everyone standing within twenty feet of the pond in a wave teeming with moss, leeches, leathery hides and short, spiky teeth.

TWENTY-FIVE

When Clint heard the gators scrambling out of the water, his first instinct was to get out of their way and let them take Rhyse and his men out of his sight. Then, almost as an afterthought, he realized something didn't fit with what he'd originally thought.

Gators?

Hadn't there only been one before?

Noticing the same thing, Joseph grabbed hold of Monique around the waist and pulled her behind him, nearly tossing her off her feet in the process. "It's a nest of 'em down there!" Joseph yelled as he jumped to Clint's side.

The edge of the pond had become alive with slithering bodies and enormous snapping jaws. Clint had to leap into the air, throwing his back against a tree to avoid getting his feet bitten clean off by the closest marauding beast. He could see Rhyse, Lovario and Stokes, but they were too busy to pose any threat. In fact, taking his eyes off the gator for just that split second was enough for the beast to move in closer.

The night erupted again, only this time with a flash of light and the explosion of Clint's shotgun, which knocked the closest gator straight back and halfway into the murky water. The bony ridges on top of the creature had been blown off by the burst of lead, which had cut away a large chunk from its back. Howling with pain and fury, the gator thrashed its body from side to side and began rolling around in the water. Its small, muscular legs kicked wildly at the ground and then the sky until it tossed itself into the pond.

"I'm out," Clint said as he opened the breech of his shotgun and popped out the spent shells.

Next to him, Ed Lovario was walking backwards while firing round after round into the body of a gator that, so far, had about eight feet of its body emerging from the water. When the pistol went off, it lit his face like a photographer's flash, illuminating the swamp in brief nightmarish glimpses.

"Clint! Look out!" Monique screamed from behind them both.

Just then, Clint saw what should have been the underbelly of the gator he'd shot. The only thing wrong was the fact that this one's belly had eyes that broke the surface of the water and a short snout that snapped down on empty air. It was yet another of the swamp creatures climbing over the body of its brother to get to the food waiting on shore.

Beside Clint, Joseph was on his knees, digging through the pouches he'd been carrying. "Here," he said to Clint. "Take this!"

Clint reached out and felt something fill his palm. Even though he couldn't see what it was, he didn't even have to look to recognize the feel of the pouch filled with shotgun shells.

Still rooting through the packs, Joseph looked quickly over to the other gator and dragged himself and the bags further away from the water. "There's got to be bullets for my pistol in here!"

While Clint was reloading his shotgun, the gator emerging from the water over the other's body opened its gaping mouth and let out a strangled hissing sound. Cold, beady eyes sat atop its skull, looking for the closest thing that it could kill and drag down beneath the water where it could be stored with the rest of the carrion it had collected.

Clint locked eyes with the scaly monster as he slipped in the second fresh shell. Knowing that Monique was somewhere right behind him, he waited until the gator was starting to crawl toward him before moving off to the side. Before he could even close the shotgun, the gator scrambled forward on quick little legs, closing the distance between them in no time at all.

Reacting on pure impulse, Clint stepped backward and then turned to the right. The gator nearly ran into Monique before she pulled herself up into one of the nearby trees. But those cold, black little eyes were riveted on Clint. For a second, the animal almost seemed angry that its prey had dared to try and run away.

Standing with one foot in the pond and the other on slippery mud, Clint snapped the shotgun closed and got ready to fire. Just as he was about to pull the trigger, the gator moved with almost unnatural speed, exposing its body that looked to be at least nine feet long. He didn't want to waste any of his ammunition, so Clint waited for the gator to close in before taking another shot.

Nearby, Lovario felt his pistol buck in his hand for the last time before the hammer fell onto an empty chamber. Still the gator came at him. The thing was dragging itself slowly on dying legs, but it had enough strength to snap out with its jaws one last time, taking a healthy bite out of its last meal.

In all his years in the swamps, Lovario had never seen a gator this big. Twelve feet of it was out of the water, and still there was more laying in the pond. Now he knew why everyone had told him to avoid this particular shore like the plague.

Waiting until the last second, Lovario jumped backward just as the gator sprung forward to clamp down with its powerful jaws. From the side of his vision, he saw a thin, bony hand press something against the top of the gator's head. There was a muffled pop and a crackle of light before something warm and wet sprayed across Lovario's face.

Bending down with pistol in hand, Mason Rhyse snarled like the creature he'd just shot while looking down at the hole he'd blown through the gator's skull. "They're right next to you," he said while pointing to Monique and Joseph. "If the beasts don't take them, make sure you do."

Lovario was too shaken up to do much else but look over at the man and woman. "Heal me, Rhyse," he begged. "I can't walk. I need you to heal me."

When Rhyse looked along the gator's long snout, he saw it had bitten down on Lovario's leg just below the knee. The reptile was still twitching convulsively in the throes of death, using every motion to bury its teeth deeper into Lovario's flesh until they were digging into his bones.

It took all of the preacher's strength to pull the gator's jaws open once it stopped moving. All he could see of the other man's leg was a slick mess of pulpy blood that looked oily and black in the moonlight. Lovario screamed while pulling himself back using just his arms. With his limb out of the gator's mouth, he could both see shards of shattered bone sticking out from the grotesque wound.

Clint waited until he could be certain the shotgun blast wouldn't catch anything but the gator's flesh before cocking back the hammer and taking quick aim. He was still backpedaling when the creature turned awkwardly toward him and began scrambling forward with the speed of a striking snake. Just as Clint was about to pull the trigger, he felt a shooting pain at the back off his ankles and suddenly the world was turned onto its ear.

His body toppled backward over a log that had been hidden beneath a carpet of moss to blend in perfectly with the rest of the shadows. When his back hit the ground, all the air was knocked out of his lungs. He couldn't feel anything but sharp pains lancing through most of his body. All he could hear was the quick, solid footsteps of the hungry gator scampering toward him.

Clint tried to sit up and fire the shotgun, but the weight of the animal was already pressing down on top of him, pinning him down beneath a solid mass of muscles and scaly flesh.

TWENTY-SIX

Clint tried to raise his arm in front of him to hold the thing back. Tried to swing the shotgun up for one shot to blow the ugly head off that gator's shoulders. The impact when the thing landed on top of him was worse than when he'd landed on the ground after stumbling over the log. The monster's breath smelled like rotten death and as its mouth opened, the thing let out an almost human groan as hot blood came pouring from its mouth.

With the shotgun held up to the gator's head, Clint stopped and realized that the heavy reptile was no longer moving. Then he saw something peeking from over the top of the animal. It was a face . . . Joseph's face. And he was smiling.

"That oughtta do it for this one," Joseph said as the animal was lifted up just enough for Clint to slide out from under it.

Once he got to his feet, Clint looked down to see Joseph straddling the nine-foot gator, his blade buried deeply into the thing's skull. He held the front half of the gator off the ground, using the embedded knife as a handle. With a quick tug, Joseph yanked the blade free and let the carcass drop heavily to the ground.

If Clint had any doubts about where Joseph's loyalties were, they disappeared at that moment.

Monique had scrambled down from her tree and was just in time to see Clint gaping at what was left of the animal that had almost swallowed him whole. "Are there any more of them?" she asked, petrified.

"I don't think we should wait around to find out," Clint said. He then put his boot on the gator's snout and gave it a kick just to make sure it was dead. The log he'd tripped over seemed to have more life in it than the animal staring up at his knees with its black, blank eyes.

Just then, they could hear the sounds of gunshots and a pained moaning coming from where Rhyse and Lovario had been standing. Clint was about to check on how the two were doing against the residents of the swamp, but something began rustling in the weeds behind Monique.

"Move," Clint barked as he reached out and pulled Monique closer to him.

Standing in the trees, glaring out like one of the demons of the bayou, was the dark, creamy face of Willie Stokes. He'd reached out to grab hold of Monique by the back of her neck, but was denied his prisoner by Clint's sudden movement. The cold, painted face of the black man twisted into a sneer, causing Joseph to jump back and away from him.

"Get out of here," Clint said as he hooked the tip of his boot under the gator's neck. "Both of you!"

Monique stayed away from the water and headed into the trees in the opposite direction from Rhyse and his men. Joseph was close behind. By the look on his face, he appeared to be more frightened of Stokes than the monstrosity he'd just taken down.

When he saw that the others were on their way, Clint brought up his leg, raising the gator's body with it. Until that moment, Stokes hadn't seen the beast laying on the ground and when Clint kicked the thing over to him, he couldn't back away fast enough. All Stokes saw was the gator coming at him and that was all he needed to see before he threw his body backwards to avoid the creature's teeth.

The gator landed like a sack of mortar, its snout grazing Stokes's foot. He quickly pulled his foot in closer and brought around the pistol he'd only recently loaded. Stokes squeezed off a shot into the gator's head and when it didn't even flinch, he thought he was soon going to be chewed up and on his back, just like Lovario.

"Did you see where—" Rhyse started to say until he noticed

the second gator sticking its nose from the weeds. He sprung up like he'd been sitting on a spring and brought his own gun around to take a shot at the animal.

They both eased up when they spotted the gaping wound at the top of the gator's skull and noticed that the thing wasn't moving. As they lowered their guns and allowed themselves to breathe normally, Rhyse and Stokes could hear nothing over the pained cries of Lovario, who was grabbing desperately at the gnarled stump that used to be his leg.

"This," Rhyse said while sweeping his arms to encompass the dead gators and Lovario's mutilated body, "is the punishment we get for failing in our mission."

"We can still find them," Lovario grunted. "Just tie up my wound and I'll track them through these swamps if I have ta crawl."

Rhyse held the pistol down to the wounded man's face and touched its barrel to his cheek. "What if I think you're a burden to us now? What if I put a bullet through your head and make sure you stay planted in this fetid mud?"

Holding out his hands and staring up at the preacher with wide, frightened eyes, Lovario began to shake from fear and blood loss. "Please, spare me. I know these swamps. I grew up here and I can lead you through them. I . . . I can figure out where they'd be headed. Please, just give me another chance!"

Stokes looked on, not knowing if he should listen to his conscience or his fears. He was just starting to raise his gun when Rhyse looked over to him with those piercing eyes. Suddenly, the fear rose up inside him and held his arm in place.

"Go after them, Stokes," Rhyse commanded. "Follow them and take them if you can. We'll catch up and help you finish them off if you need us. And don't be stupid. If you get close enough you put a bullet into them. Their backs, their brains, their chests, it doesn't matter. Dead is dead. There ain't no honor in these swamps and there ain't no such thing as a fair fight. Kill them any way you can, unnerstand?"

"Yessir," Stokes said with a solemn nod. "I would'a come around in front of them if they hadn't stopped here. They would'a walked right into me."

"Well go do it again. And if you kill even one of them, I'll let you see your family again."

A smile drifted onto Stokes's face, soon to be replaced by a shadow of regret. "If that's what I got to do."

Rhyse looked down to check on the tourniquet he was trying around Lovario's leg. When he looked back up again, Stokes was gone. Smiling, Rhyse cinched in the knot extra tight until he felt Lovario squirm on the ground and bite his lip to hold back a yelp of pain.

Always good to keep them scared and hurt, Rhyse thought. That made it easier for them to close their eyes and follow orders so they could let someone else take care of them. It worked on the men who did his bidding the same way it worked on all the people paralyzed by their superstition.

Kneeling there on the ground, surrounded by the corpses of beasts and his hands soaked in blood, Rhyse actually felt like he'd earned the priest's collar he wore. He had become a taker of life and a healer as well. The bayou was a dangerous place and had taken its best shot at him, only to fail.

"I am the master of this land," he said to himself while pouring water from his own canteen over Lovario's wound. "And I am its dark, twisted soul."

Something snapped in Rhyse's head at that moment. Even without partaking of his own blend of drugged whiskey, he started believing all the things he'd been preaching. Everything he thought was so much smoke being blown in the name of a good scam suddenly didn't seem so farfetched.

He had become the most dangerous kind of foe: a madman who fully believed his own stream of lies.

TWENTY-SEVEN

Joseph dug a box of matches out of one of the packs he carried and used them to light a torch Clint had fashioned out of a damp stick and strips torn from pieces of all their clothing. Most of what was burning came from the bottom of Joseph's coat and the flickering light made every shadow jump at them. Soon, Monique began to point them in the right direction and eventually found a crude path.

"Believe it or not," she said, "but this is starting to look familiar."

"Have you been here before?" Clint asked.

"A few times, but I came in from a completely different direction. There's a few people living nearby."

"A town?"

"Not hardly. Not unless you think four crooked shacks in a row is a town."

Joseph stopped and turned around. "How far is it to those shacks?"

"Can't tell you for sure. Like I said, I only been there a few times. And even then I needed a guide."

Joseph gestured in front of them with the torch. "Well that way is north. Do you remember how to get there from Jespin?"

Clint scanned the bayou behind them, looking for any trace of another torch. He strained his ears trying to search for any other footsteps, human or otherwise, coming in from the dark. Besides the normal chatter of the swamp life, there was nothing to worry about. "This place has got to be north of Jespin if she recognizes this area." Turning to Monique, he asked, "Did you have to cross the river?"

She thought for a second. "No."

"Then that rules out west."

They continued along the trail. Sometimes it took all three of them to keep sight of the path when it became overrun with growth or washed out by the overflowing bog. Not once did they catch sight of Rhyse or his men, or even hear another person's footsteps. Eventually, Joseph spotted something in the darkness up ahead.

"Take a look here, Miss Monique," he whispered, waving her forward. "That look familiar?"

Monique came up beside Joseph and peered into the murky blackness. Finally, she saw what he'd seen: a small cluster of windows burning dimly with well-kept fires. "That's it. I'll be sure when we get a little closer, but that's got to be it."

"You two go on ahead," Clint said. "I want to stay out here to make sure there's nobody following us. The last thing I want to do is lead Rhyse to another group of people he can terrorize."

Monique started to protest, but came back to Clint's side and wrapped her arms around him instead. "Be careful," she said while pressing her body closely against his. Her breath was warm and intoxicating on his neck and her hands rubbed the muscles in his back.

Clint started walking with them toward the buildings, but when they moved around a large tree, he stayed behind and ducked into the cover of the thick foliage. Slowly, quietly, he worked his way through the swamp, backtracking until he was in a position to see anything that walked or slithered by the trail on its way to where Monique and Joseph were waiting.

He sat hidden in the brush until he could feel the mud slipping between his toes. After a few minutes, Clint became accustomed to the constant chatter of the insects and the weird songs of the toads. Looking up, he could see patches of stars where the ceiling of overhanging vines broke up overhead.

Just as he was starting to develop a better attitude toward the bayou, Clint heard the rustling of footsteps in the distance. Another gator was making its way back to the water. Either it didn't know Clint was nearby or it didn't care because it kept on walking until it eventually plunked into a wet spot and stayed there.

Getting up to stretch his legs, Clint checked his bearings and headed a little deeper into the bog. He'd just lost sight of the path when he heard something that resembled the swift rhythm of footsteps. The sound was a light brushing aside of leaves and the occasional snap of a twig. Clint hunkered down, using an old stump for cover.

For a moment, the noise stopped. Knowing better than to take the silence for granted, Clint kept still until his knees started to burn and his back began to get stiff from keeping his body bunched up for so long. Finally, the noise came back. Then it drew closer.

When Stokes snuck into the small clearing, Clint thought he'd been spotted for sure. Instead, the tall black man scanned the shadows and looked right past Clint's position. After sitting and listening for a few seconds, Stokes moved on and headed in the opposite direction of the buildings Monique had found.

Satisfied, Clint headed to meet the others.

Maneuvering through the darkness on his way back to the small settlement, Clint found he'd become much better at recognizing one piece of boggy marsh from another. Just as he'd taught himself how to find his way among the ranges and prairies while on the trail, the bayou had its own way of letting him know where he should or shouldn't step. He was even able to pick out a few landmarks once he concentrated on every piece of his surroundings rather than think of them as one big whole.

Before long, he was in sight of the few buildings that had been set up in a relatively clear patch of land next to what appeared to be a freshwater stream. It was hard to tell in the dark, but Clint was unable to see the usual growth floating on top of the water. He didn't trust his instincts enough to take a drink from the stream, but he figured it would have to be clean water for anyone to build their homes next to it.

Monique hadn't been exaggerating when she'd said there were only four buildings in the group. Two of them resembled lodges that Clint had seen up north with slanted roofs and a small chimney jutting from the side. The other two buildings were two floors tall and about half the size of the saloon back in Byers. Even though the second floors on them seemed to be leaning at a slight angle, the wood looked so weathered that Clint figured they'd make it through many more hard seasons before toppling over.

One of the two-level buildings had an elaborate contraption alongside it that was made up of metal tubs, a pump and copper tubing. When he walked up closer to it, Clint was almost knocked over by the potent smell of alcohol. Apparently, the residents here took to brewing their own moonshine rather than trudge through miles of swamps to get drunk in town. Clint couldn't blame them. After the day he'd had, he could use a drink himself.

He leaned over the still and took another whiff of the stuff inside. Almost instantly, the hairs in his nose started to curl and he felt a serious burning in his throat. On the other hand, he figured, he should probably stick to a beer if he could find one.

"Thank the lord, you're back," came a familiar voice from just around the corner.

Grabbing hold of Clint's arm, Monique spun him around until she could press her body firmly against his. Her arms snaked around his waist and the heat from her skin made Clint feel hot and anxious. In the pale moonlight, she looked even more exotic. The smooth contours of her rich, dark skin glistened with beads of sweat that ran down her shoulders and neck to form little glittering trails. Every piece of clothing she wore stuck to her flesh like a transparent film.

As if sensing his eyes upon her, Monique backed away a few steps and let her head roll forward demurely. The beads in her hair rattled together when she turned to look up at him and a smile turned up the edges of her thick, full lips. "I talked to the man who called for me last time I was here," she said. "He'll let us stay in his extra room."

"What about Joseph?"

Monique shrugged, the motion shifting her body beneath the thin material that clung to her like another skin. She reached out to take Clint's hand and guide it over her firm breasts while staring straight up into his eyes. "He's staying with someone else. I could have had him stay closer, but . . . I wanted you to myself tonight."

When she let go of him, Clint's hands stayed right where

she'd left them. Monique closed her eyes and arched her head back, savoring the feel of him cupping her breasts and gently rubbing her large, hard nipples.

"Is this the work of one of your mother's love potions?" Clint asked as she led him toward a set of stairs going up the back of the building.

Giggling mischievously, Monique opened a door at the top of the stairs which led directly into a small bedroom. "If it is, it's been driving me crazy since the minute you walked into my house." She kissed him fully on the mouth, her tongue probing as he worked his hands over her breasts.

"Remind me to thank her when we get back," Clint said as he peeled the dress down off Monique's shoulders.

TWENTY-EIGHT

As the thin material slipped down Monique's body, Clint could feel his fingertips tracing over her smooth, silky skin. Her dark body moved sensuously in the shadows as she reached out to start removing Clint's shirt. When the dress came down over her rounded hips, she squirmed until it dropped to her feet.

Once again, she reached out to grab hold of Clint's wrists and moved his hands over her body. First, she slid them over her breasts and then down both sides, lingering so he could massage the muscles in her hips. "I've been wanting to feel you touch me since you first looked at me," she whispered. "Now, I don't want you to take your hands from my skin."

Leaning back, Monique moved his hands further down until his palms grazed the patch of moist hair between her legs. "Mmmm," she purred. "Right there." She then moved one of his hands between her thighs until his fingertips traced lightly over the sensitive skin which parted to allow him to feel inside. "And there."

She pressed in closer to him, her eyes wide and anxious. Monique's little tongue darted out to lick her lips as she urged his fingers deep inside her. When Clint began moving them in and out, she started breathing in quick gasps, her grip on his wrists getting tighter as if to make sure he didn't even think of stopping.

Her hips started to make little thrusting motions in time with the rhythm of his hand, finally letting his wrists go so she

116

could reach out and tug at his belt. While undressing him, she wriggled her body so that he was touching her in just the right spots. Monique slid her hands beneath Clint's pants and pulled them down so she could reach down and stroke his hard shaft. Most of the mud that had covered them had been on their clothes, and it was all in a pile on the floor, now.

"Oh God, Clint, keep doing it just like that," she moaned with her head leaning back and her eyes clamped shut.

The way she stood there as he pleasured her made Clint think of an exotic tribal dance. Her knees began to tremble and her hips thrust against his fingers, driving him deeper and deeper inside her. All the while, her hands were wrapped around his pole, gripping gently and squeezing with the rhythm of her motion. Their bodies were close enough that Clint could smell the musky scent of her sex and could feel the moisture dripping down her leg.

Grunting as she moved her hips, she held Clint's cock in both hands and stroked it in long, slow movements. Her own body was being taken over by her pleasure and when her hips stopped thrusting, her moans grew to a wild shout. Clint moved his fingers inside her and tickled the soft nub of flesh just over her opening until Monique's eyelids began to flutter and her breath caught in her throat.

Soon, every muscle in her body tightened and her hands wrapped around his cock so that he could feel the tremors as they wracked her body. When her eyes opened, Monique reached down to once again hold Clint's wrist. She slid his fingers out of her, raised them to her mouth and wrapped her lips around them so she could suck her own juices off his skin.

She licked every drop off of him and smiled as though savoring her taste. Now it was Clint's turn to take her by the hand and lead her to the bed. His rigid pole was aching to be inside of her and he wanted nothing more at that moment than to feel her body dance beneath his.

Her lithe figure slid through the shadows just as his fingers had slid between her lips and when Monique sat down on the edge of the bed, she reached down and spread herself open for him. Even in the darkness, he could see the contrast of her ebony skin and the glistening wet pink between her legs. Clint reached down to grab her rounded buttocks and Monique

leaned back so she could lift her rump off the bed until her
sex was pressing against the head of his cock.

Clint couldn't keep the moan from coming out as he buried
himself deep inside her. Propping herself up with her hands
behind her, Monique stared at him hungrily, wrapping her legs
around his back so she could lock them around his waist. He
thrust his pole between her thighs and moved his hips in little
circles to hit all the spots he'd felt moments ago.

Every motion brought a gasp from Monique's lips and soon
she was moving her own hips in time with their rhythm. Along
with the passionate groaning, the sound of their flesh pounding
together filled the room. Each little impact drove him deeper
inside until he was about to explode.

"Come on, baby," Monique grunted. "Do it for me."

"Not yet," Clint said as he pulled out of her. "I'm not
through with you."

Monique got to her knees and threw her arms around Clint's
neck. She showered him with kisses and then twisted her body
to pull him off balance. She playfully forced him down to the
bed and then put her hands on his chest to knead her fingers
over his muscles.

Clint stretched out and enjoyed the feeling of her climbing
on top of him, slithering against his body to rub her erect
nipples against his legs and then between them. Crouching
down at the foot of the bed, Monique leaned down and pushed
her breasts around Clint's rod. Then she moved her body up
and down, teasing him with the feel of her smooth flesh rubbing against his rigid column of flesh.

Before long, she lowered her mouth over his cock and consumed him in long, slow bobs of her head. Monique reached
up to rake her nails down Clint's stomach as she sucked him.
Her tongue swirled expertly around his tip and she gripped his
hips so she could begin vigorously going down on him.

Running his fingers through her tightly braided hair, Clint
pulled her head up and urged her to crawl back on top of him.
She did so eagerly and soon impaled herself on his shaft, riding
it hard as she clasped her hands behind her head while arching
her back. From where he was, Clint got a perfect view of
Monique's round, full breasts as she bounced on top of him.

He could feel the lips between her legs gripping him tighter
and soon Monique leaned forward so she could thrust her hips

back and forth. She rode his cock using her knees to move her hips up and down, continuing the sensual dance until Clint had to grab hold of her soft rear and drive himself inside deep and hard.

Now, Monique and Clint were moaning in unison and when the climax overtook them, their bodies clenched around each other as if they would never be able to let go. Finally, she rolled off so she could curl up in his arms with her head resting on Clint's chest.

"This must be our reward for the hell we've had to go through to get here," she whispered while gently running her fingers over Clint's body.

"You know, I would have been more than happy to reward you in my room back in Byers and we could have avoided all the gators."

"You may think I'm crazy, but everything feels different now. Almost like my body is celebrating being alive."

Clint rolled onto his side to face her and slid his hands over the curving slope of her hips. Almost without thinking about it, Monique shifted to open her legs for him and sighed luxuriously as his fingers played over her sensitive folds.

"I think I've got some more celebrating to do," Clint said as he moved down to flick his tongue over her nipples.

TWENTY-NINE

Clint woke just as dawn was making its presence known in the bayou. The glass on his window was steamed up from the almost tropical humidity and when he walked over to look outside, he realized he hadn't seen much of his room before he'd become occupied with better things.

The bed was just big enough for Clint and Monique to share comfortably, and it was pushed up against a wall that was made from warped and splintered planks of wood. There was a washbasin below the window and further inside the room was a small round table with three rickety chairs pushed beneath it. Already, Clint could hear the sounds of people moving about downstairs and was almost too embarrassed to go down and introduce himself after the noise he'd made the night before.

When Clint's stomach began to churn and the smell of frying bacon hit his nose, however, he decided that hunger was always enough to win out over modesty. He went to wake up Monique, but she was sleeping so peacefully, he couldn't get himself to shake her. Instead, he slipped on his clothes and headed for the door which led to the outside stairs. Most of the mud that had been on his clothes was now lying in dried clumps on the floor.

Waiting at the bottom, standing next to the pieced-together still, was Joseph Terray. He watched Clint as though he didn't know if he should take a shot at him or ask to join him for breakfast.

Clint gave a friendly wave and walked around the building to go in through the front door. Joseph followed him in. The inside looked identical to the room upstairs, complete with a small desk and a large bed. Further inside, however, was a kitchen and small dining area.

"Who the hell is out dere?" came a high-pitched voice that sounded as though a cat was being shredded into ragged pieces.

Poking his head from a large cabinet set up in the middle of the room as a divider, a small, pear-shaped man waddled around to eye Clint and Joseph suspiciously. "You'd be the new folks 'round here, eh?"

Tipping his hat, Clint said, "Yessir. I didn't get a chance to thank you for your hospitality when I got in last night. My name's Clint Adams."

The rotund man was a full head shorter than Clint, but probably still outweighed him by a good fifty pounds. Extending a rough, dirty hand, he turned his head to shoot a wad of brown water from his mouth and into a spittoon sitting near the bed. "I'm Stu and that there in the kitchen is m'wife, Ellen."

A tall woman who looked about as shapely as a coatrack was standing in front of a pot-bellied stove. Hearing her name, she waved and started giggling loudly. "Which one'a you was upstairs with Miss Monique?" she asked.

"That'd be me," Clint said.

"I'll bet you worked up a big appetite."

Thinking back to the noise he and Monique had made throughout the night, Clint nodded and felt his cheeks flushing with color. "Sorry about that."

"No need for that," Ellen said. "Actually, it was nice to hear someone up in that old room. Ever since our boy left home, we ain't never had any guests around. 'Sides, you two helped inspire my Stu to—"

"Alright, Ellen," Stu scolded while shrugging apologetically to Clint. "I'm sure they don't wanna hear none'a that."

Clint tried to think about the delicious smells coming from the kitchen before his appetite was completely ruined by the images Ellen had put into his head. Looking behind him, he actually saw Joseph smiling and shaking his head. It was the first glimpse of the man he'd once known that Clint had seen since leaving Byers a year ago.

"Miss Monique did wonders for a nasty bug that was goin' round these parts last time she was through here," Stu continued. "She got us all feelin' better right quick, so I figure the least we can do is put y'all up for the night and fill your bellies. My wife's one helluva cook."

"I can tell," Clint said while taking a deep smell of the warm air. The buttery aroma of fresh biscuits floated through the room, along with the smell of grits and of course the bacon that had brought him downstairs in the first place.

Suddenly, the door behind Joseph opened and Monique peeked inside to get a sample of the cooking smells for herself. Clint noticed that her hair was a little mussed and her clothes were only loosely buttoned around her. She walked past them and into the kitchen as though she was at home, striking up a conversation with Ellen that quickly became a lot of whispering, giggling and glancing in Clint's direction. Clint felt himself blush, which he found both odd and amazing.

Ellen made a bucket of water available to all three of them and they washed the swamp off them as much as they could before sitting down to breakfast. Clint wondered when he'd get a chance to take a proper bath. He also wondered about Eclipse. He wasn't sure where the Darley Arabian was right now. If some harm had come to the horse there was going to be hell to pay for sure.

"Well, come on and have a seat," Stu offered while dragging Clint and Joseph toward a large dining table in the kitchen. "After all, I'm sure you want to get yerselves fed and on yer way before you waste too much of this fine day."

With the sun just barely a smudge on the horizon, it was plain that Stu was a generous man who felt more than a little nervous at the thought of keeping his guests around for very much longer. Clint watched Joseph and the way he moved about like someone who'd been dropped down from the sky. He smelled the food that was set in front of him as though he'd never expected to experience something so normal as a meal again. Even when he looked at Stu and Ellen, he seemed to be waiting for them to scream or cry in fear.

Clint watched Joseph as the man ate ravenously. When he

topped off his second helping of grits, he started to look different. Clint couldn't quite put his finger on it, but something was changing inside Joseph Terray. Almost like he was coming back to life again.

THIRTY

Joseph was busy trying to clean out Ellen's kitchen for good when Clint and Monique slipped outside so they could talk in private. They walked in front of the house and down what loosely resembled a street until they stood on the edge of the encroaching swamp. Monique seemed to lose her smile the closer she got to the line of trees.

"I'm afraid, Clint," she said quietly.

He reached his arm around her and drew her in close to his side. "We'll make it out of this, I swear. Besides, I can't lose you. I need you to show me the way back to my horse so I can ride as far away from these damn swamps as I can."

She laughed nervously and huddled in close to him. "I don't know if we can trust Joseph anymore. He's probably found a way to tell Rhyse about us."

"I've been thinking about that and I have the feeling that he's not as far gone as you think. After all, he did help save our lives last night."

"He was saving his own life. I can tell just by lookin' at him that he's not the same man."

Clint broke away from her and put his foot up on a mossy old stump. "After what he's been through, you're probably right. Hell, I've had a pretty good taste of what Rhyse does to his men and I may not be the same for a while either."

Pacing around for a few seconds, Monique scanned the bayou carefully for any signs of Rhyse and his men. Clint was doing the same thing, but his was more of a concentrated search. He kept his eyes trained on one spot while keeping himself aware for any movement in his field of vision. This way, he could watch a huge chunk of the area at once.

Every time a leaf was moved aside by a passing lizard or a tree branch swung beneath the weight of the occasional bird or small bat, his eyes shot in that direction and his stomach tensed in anticipation of the coming gunshot. The longer he stayed in that spot, the more he wanted to go back upstairs and get the shotgun. It still felt awkward in his hands compared to his own gun, but . . .

"Hey, Clint," came a voice from the front of Stu's house.

Clint had heard the door slam shut and was already turning around by the time Joseph had called his name, but he was still nervous enough to feel startled by the sudden sound. "What is it, Joseph?" he asked.

Joseph was starting to get some color in his skin and a bit of spring in his walk. He had one of the packs he'd been carrying slung over his shoulder and when he got closer to Clint, he reached inside to pull out something Clint had been anxious to see.

"I'll bet you've been missing this," Joseph said as he took out Clint's gun belt and held it out for him. "One of the people back in Jespin handed this over before we left. I wasn't there in town, but they gave it to me to lug around for them."

Clint took it, strapped the familiar leather around his waist and checked to make sure his custom pistol was loaded. Every cylinder was full. Snapping the chamber shut with a flick of his thumb, Clint slid the gun home and felt a lot better about the way things had been shaping up. "Thanks, Joseph. Now what about you? How's it feel to be away from Rhyse and his group of crazies?"

Joseph took a quick breath. "He ain't crazy and neither are Lovario or Stokes."

"So you really think Rhyse brought them and you all back from the grave?"

"I did up until a few hours ago, but a dead man can't eat that good. And besides," he added while looking over to Monique, "she wouldn't stand for no walking corpse bein' so close to her. I seen what she could do and Miss Monique

would've been able to get away a long time ago if that's all
we were."

Monique nodded solemnly. "The dead got better things to
do than the evil that Rhyse is responsible for." Reaching out
to take Joseph's hand, she placed her fingertips on his wrist
and squeezed tight. "I can feel the blood pumping through your
veins. An' I can see the goodness in your eyes. Now more
than ever."

Clint gave her a doubting look to which Monique shook her
head. "I thought you were corrupted too much to be saved,
but you've proven yourself more than enough." When she put
her arms around Joseph in a loving hug, Monique rubbed his
back like a comforting mother or a priest giving comfort to
one in need.

"Glad you decided to come back to the land of the living,
Joseph," Clint said as he gave the man a pat on the shoulder.
"Now let's stick together and then we'll have a better chance
of making it out of these stinking swamps alive."

Also, Clint thought, it would make it a whole lot easier to
keep an eye on those who needed watching.

Mason Rhyse sat with his back against a soggy log and his
legs sprawled out in the mud. Throughout the night, he'd been
feeling his body sink into the ground by half an inch every
few hours or so. He'd closed his eyes, planning where he could
go next and what he should do, wondering if it was worth
bringing Ed Lovario back from the dead a second time.

Opening his eyes again, Rhyse could detect the color in the
sky changing from star-speckled black to a dark gray. Clench-
ing his fist, he gripped Lovario's shirt and felt the dead man's
skin squish beneath his fingers. Lovario still gazed up at the
sky with his glazed-over eyes.

"What you lookin' at, Ed?" Rhyse asked the corpse. "You
starin' up at the angels or takin' one last look before you got
dragged down into the pit?"

Rhyse's hand moved along Lovario's shoulder and up to the
blackened hole in his skull. Touching the wound made Rhyse
think about the night before and all the screaming that had
come out of Ed's mouth when they'd tried to keep moving
through the bayou. Rhyse had pulled the man along behind
him like a sack of mortar and Lovario hadn't done anything

but get heavier. He remembered setting Lovario down and looking down at him with disgust. The resurrected soul had become a sniveling baby all because of some wound in his flesh.

He'd promised to heal him. Lovario had made him promise when they'd been tramping through the night that when they could rest, Rhyse would heal him and make the pain stop. They'd trudged even farther and Rhyse told him he'd help him. Even when the few remaining tendons holding on to Lovario's foot had snapped, Rhyse kept dragging him.

"I'll go back for it, Ed," he'd promised.

But he never did. He'd let that foot drop off like an old shoe and didn't even bother trying to remember where it had landed. Finally, Rhyse couldn't carry him any further. He found a spot big enough for both of them to sit in and that's just what they did. Everything would have been fine if Lovario would've stopped his screaming.

All night long, he'd been screaming as if the nerves in his body still worked and he could feel the damage that gator had done. But dead men weren't supposed to feel anything and as the pain got worse, Lovario began to realize that he was very much alive.

They all came to their senses eventually. Rhyse had put plenty of men through these paces and they all saw through the sham eventually. So, like he'd done for the others when that realization came, Rhyse put his gun against the doubter's head and emptied his brains onto the ground.

Now, with his fingers lightly tracing over the puckered hole in Lovario's head, Rhyse imagined that he really did have the power over life and death. Something in the back of his mind told him that what had started out as a scam to scare superstitious locals had actually grown into a true skill. Maybe he could use his gift for real.

Maybe he could hold back the reaper with his raised hand and pull a man from his grave. Not one that was merely sleeping and covered with dirt, but a man who'd really met his maker.

Rhyse placed his palms on Lovario's temples, feeling the cold touch of death on the man's soggy flesh. He started to chant. Although he didn't know what to say, Rhyse made something up the way he always did and imagined the skin getting warmer and those eyes turning in their sockets to look at him with thanks.

He chanted until the sun poked its head up to start the day and when it shone down on them, it was still shining down upon a dead man and a liar.

Rhyse stopped his chanting and shrugged.

Maybe next time.

THIRTY-ONE

When they were alone, Clint and Monique went back up to their room to gather what little they had before heading back into the bayou.

"I need you to do me a favor," Clint said while counting up his bullets and tending to the guns.

Monique was trying to get some of the dirt from her clothes even though a fresh layer of grime would be applied the instant she stepped into the bog. "You don't have to ask, just name it."

"I need you to perform an exorcism."

Monique dropped what she was doing and turned to face Clint. "And all this time, I thought you didn't believe in the power of the spirits."

"It would be for Rhyse's men. I think if we can get them to believe they're no longer under his control, we can get them away from him before they get killed."

"Rhyse is a powerful man. It might not be that easy."

"Powerful?" Clint scoffed. "He's just a con man using fear to get people to follow him. He uses that same fear to pave the way for himself whenever he rides into the next town and starts making demands."

A flash of anger showed on Monique's face. When she balled up her fists and propped them on her hips, she looked an awful lot like her mother. "You may think I'm stupid, Clint, but I'm not. Jus' because I don't practice medicine like your doctors up north, I still help these people. I help a lot of people."

"I know that, Monique. All I'm saying is that Rhyse is using spiritualism and voodoo to put on a show that is convincing enough to get people to follow him to their deaths. I know because I was in one of those shows in case you don't remember and if I'd have been a believer in that stuff to begin with, I might have been scared enough to follow Rhyse, too."

The anger in Monique's eyes started to fade. Crossing her arms in front of herself, she turned so she could look out the window. "I just don't want you to think that what he does is the same as what I do. Rhyse gets his power from those shows he puts on. I could see into the eyes of those other two and they've been around him too long to go back." Turning to face him, she added, "Joseph was one thing, but I don't think anyone could bring them others back."

"Well, I've got an idea, but it'll take both of us for it to work. First we need to get back to that estate and make sure Rhyse doesn't return for his prisoner."

"He doesn't have to go back there," Monique said. "He can take his pick of any of those estates an' they'll all gladly pay to keep his evil spirits away from their family."

"Well we're going there anyway to get my horse. I've about had my fill of walking everywhere."

They finished their preparations in silence. Clint oiled the guns and loaded them, filling his pockets with as many spare rounds as he could while Monique did her best to try not to think about the day that lay ahead. Once Clint was ready to move out, he walked up behind Monique and turned her around so he could look her in the eye.

"I never got an answer from you about whether or not you'd help me," he said.

She held her chin up high, even though she was obviously nervous about going back out where Rhyse was waiting. "I'm no witch doctor, but I'll do my best."

"All you have to do is convince them that you know what you're doing. Nothing fancy, just something that looks good. Joseph seems fine one minute and confused the next. All he needs is a push in the right direction."

A little smirk played across Monique's lips. "What's cooking inside that head of yours? Or do I even want to know?"

"It's something that can hopefully let those men with Rhyse go back to their families before they get killed."

"And what about Rhyse, himself?"

Clint picked up the sawed-off shotgun from where it had been laying on the bed atop a folded cloth. "That depends on him. He'll either be going to jail or into one of those holes in the ground he seems so fond of. Doesn't really matter to me which one."

She reached up to put both hands on Clint's face and held him close so that when she spoke, he could feel her lips brushing against his own. "You jus' watch yourself," she said as some of her accent began to re-assert itself. "Mother would kill me if I came back without you."

Joseph was waiting for them as they came down the stairs. A gun was strapped to his side. Although his expression was somewhat haunted, he looked ready for the long day ahead of them. Clint walked up to him and put a hand on his shoulder.

"You look a lot better when you're not playing dead," Clint said.

"Yeah, well I've been thinking about the last few days and I feel awful foolish. After being played for an idiot and followin' the likes of Mason Rhyse, I don't know if I want to show my face back in Byers at all."

"If you're not planning on going back let me know so I can break the news to Kim when I see her."

At the mention of his wife's name, Joseph's face brightened. "You saw her? Is she all right?"

"She misses you, but I think we can fix that."

Suddenly, Joseph's happiness dimmed as though a cloud had passed over the sun. "If she'll have me. She's not the type to settle down with an outlaw."

Laughing, Clint said, "From what I saw, you didn't do much by way of breaking any laws out there. Scared a few locals, maybe, but at least you didn't kill any of them."

Joseph shook his head. "I guess you're right, but I feel . . . I don't know . . . like Rhyse did something to me. The way he talked and those things he said . . ." His words drifted off and he stared out into the swamps like he could still smell the dirt packed in around his body and hear Rhyse's insane chanting about the devil pulling him from the grave.

Just then, Monique walked up behind him and gently moved Clint aside. "Here," she said soothingly. "Let me do something for you before we go." To Clint, she gave a subtle nod before leading Joseph to a quiet place next to a small well at the end of the road.

Clint watched as Monique got Joseph to kneel down with her and close his eyes. From there, she started to chant and hold her hands on his forehead in what, for all Clint could tell, was a legitimate ceremony of some kind. She took a handful of mud and rubbed it on her hands while leaning her head back so she could direct her voice up to the breaking dawn. Then she took her hands and placed them over Joseph's heart.

They sat there for a few seconds, not even noticing the doors and windows that had opened and the people watching them from their homes. Soon, they both got to their feet and Monique said something softly to Joseph. When he answered, Joseph smiled widely and lightly touched the mud on his hands.

Monique walked back to Clint and wiped her hands clean on a rag that had been tied around her neck. "You were right," she said, "I really do think I can help Rhyse's men."

"What was all that?" Clint asked.

"Nothing really. To him, though, it was a ritual to cleanse his soul from all the evil that Rhyse had inflicted."

Clint looked over to Joseph who seemed to stand straight and ready for anything. "I'd say it worked. You do that to Lovario and Stokes and they won't have any reason to do what Rhyse tells him."

"First we need to get them to want to go through with it."

"I've almost got that part worked out. For now, let's get moving before everyone in this place wants their soul cleansed, too."

Monique said her goodbyes to Stu and Ellen, waving to them as she, Joseph and Clint started walking into the bayou. Everyone looking out from their doors or windows watched Monique as though she'd brought rain to a desert. They reminded Clint of a congregation after a particularly uplifting sermon. Their eyes were wide and their faces were happy.

An honest-to-goodness miracle had been performed in their eyes and Clint was beginning to think they were right. There was definitely something about Monique and the way she affected the energy of those around her. He wasn't even sure if

it could be called voodoo, but whatever it was, he just hoped
it would be enough to turn around Rhyse's men.

If not, he'd just have to do his best to try and get them out
of the bayou alive.

THIRTY-TWO

Crouching in the damp muck, getting chewed up by mosquitoes bigger than his thumb, Stokes tried not to think about the pain in his knees after having sat in the same position for hours on end. He tried not to think about the hunger gnawing at his stomach. And most of all, he tried not to think about the sight of Mason Rhyse sitting over the mutilated body of Ed Lovario.

He'd gone to Rhyse a few hours before dawn so he could tell him where Joseph and the others were spending the night. Stokes had had to do some backtracking, but once he'd found the small cluster of ramshackle buildings, it was only a matter of time before he'd caught sight of his prey through a window. When he found Rhyse, the preacher was stretched out in the mud with his hand resting on Lovario's face. Swarms of flies were already thick around the corpse, but Rhyse didn't seem to notice and told him to keep an eye on the buildings until first light.

Now, with first light changing the color of the sky to a brilliant orange, Stokes shifted his position in the weeds and watched as Miss Monique performed her magic on Joseph. Stokes didn't know what was going on, but he did know that Monique was a woman of power and whatever she was doing seemed to be opening Joseph's eyes.

Stokes shifted around so that he was facing away from the buildings and slowly made his way into the bush. Once he was far enough into the swamp, he raised up to his full height and started running to the spot where he'd last seen Rhyse. When he got there, all Stokes found was the body of Ed Lovario.

In his time with Rhyse, Stokes had seen his share of dead bodies. But those were fresh kills and a few of them were even well enough to walk and talk the next day. He hadn't seen anything like this.

Lovario had been laying there for less than twelve hours and already the creatures of the swamp were breaking off pieces and carrying them away. Insects of all shapes and sizes skittered over Lovario's flesh and a pair of enormous beetles were scraping at his open, staring eyes. The stump that had once been his leg was black and already starting to show signs of mold. Leeches had attached to the open wounds and a lizard chewed on Ed's fingers.

Before he could turn away, Stokes felt the bile rising up in his throat. When he tried to take in a breath of air and got a nose full of the rotting stench, he staggered away from the remains, dropped to his hands and knees and vomited until the muscles in his stomach were sore from overexertion.

"This is death," came a voice from a few feet away.

Stokes wiped his mouth with the back of his hand and looked up to find Rhyse standing there gazing down at him. Reflexively, Stokes scrambled to his feet, careful not to look anywhere near the corpse.

There was a fresh coat of pale paste on Rhyse's skin which meant that he was planning on something happening real soon. In a harsh voice, he said, "I can tell you got a good look. And that's good, because if you fail me like Lovario did, you'll end up like him only worse."

"I won't fail you," Stokes said shakily. "I even know where they's headed."

Rhyse nodded, but didn't lose any of the intensity in his eyes. "Let me ask you something. Did you see Lovario's face?"

Stokes tried to answer, but had to nod slowly when he found he couldn't get the words out.

"His eyes were wide open and he was staring up in agony, praying for someone to release his soul so he didn't have to feel the scavengers partaking of his flesh. That's what happens to those who fail me. I can make sure that you'll be stuck in that body of yours even when it's rotting away around you."

The roar of the cicadas filled their ears, but to Stokes it was the sound of tiny insect claws scraping against dry bone.

"I . . . I won't fail you, Mistah Rhyse."

"That's good, because we need to hunt those traitors down and get rid of them before that young woman is able to get home to her mother. If Madame Cleo is given enough time, that witch can send us all to hell."

I saw Miss Monique doin' somethin' to Joseph," Stokes said after an uncomfortable silence.

Rhyse's eyebrows went up and he tilted his head in interest. "Go on."

The black man explained everything he'd seen while watching the buildings through the night and explained in full detail the ceremony he'd witnessed just before Clint, Monique and Joseph had headed back into the swamp.

"That's interesting," Rhyse said after Stokes had finished talking. "And here I thought Cleo's daughter was nothing more than an errand girl who made deliveries and did the occasional healing where it was needed. Looks like Monique has grown into a more powerful witch than I'd thought."

"It looked like she was h . . . helping Joseph. He looked . . . happy afterward."

Before Stokes could blink, he felt a stinging blow across his jaw that sent a jolt of rage through his system. His instincts kept his body from reacting, but had a harder time when Rhyse hit him again.

The preacher stared into Stokes's eyes and even though he had to look up to do it, Rhyse still gave the impression that he stood a mile above the other man. "You're a fool! All she did was twist his mind until he agreed to follow her. She won't do nothin' for Joseph besides turn him against us."

After a few seconds, the anger in both men dwindled away to nothing. Rhyse snapped his head around in response to a sound that Stokes had heard almost a full minute ago. "They're headed this way," Rhyse whispered. Before Stokes could step aside, Rhyse added, "You done good. I'm sorry for striking you, but you can't let yourself be fooled by them deceivers. You gotta be strong and kill Joseph the next time you see him."

"What about Miss Monique? You ain't gonna hurt her, are you?"

"Of course not," Rhyse promised. His mind was racing at the possibilities of getting his hands on someone like Monique. So many towns would pay to have their beloved healer back among them. Every person in Byers would pool their money to pay for her safe return.

"But that's not to say that the ones with Monique won't hurt her," Rhyse added.

That caught Stokes's attention and put an angry snarl on his face. "Why would they do that?"

"Because she's no longer useful to them."

"So do we go after them now?"

"No. They almost got eaten up by the swamp yesterday and they'll probably get lost or killed today without us havin' to bother with 'em. We got a new day ahead of us. It's as good a time as any to finish up the job we came here for."

Stokes led the way back to the trail that would take them to the Zeller estate. It would be hours before they got there and that time passed in complete silence. Even though he didn't say a word, Rhyse was busy working himself up into a fit of energy that would explode at the first provocation.

Seeing the preacher's eyes turn cold and piercing, Stokes knew the day would end in a mess of blood. He'd seen Rhyse like this before.

It was never pretty.

THIRTY-THREE

Tramping through the wet mud and breathing in the moldy air was actually starting to feel familiar to Clint. It wasn't exactly the kind of familiarity he enjoyed, but the bayou was becoming less and less of a foreign land to him. The night before, he'd developed a sense of direction in the soggy wilderness and now that he could see more than ten feet in front of him, Clint was almost able to lead the way back to Zeller's estate outside of Jespin.

When they were less than a mile away, they found a small clearing well away from the path and took a few minutes to rest their feet. Monique ran her fingers through her hair, wringing sweat from her braids as if it was rain. The closer they'd gotten, the more nervous Joseph had become. Now, he sat still and quiet, preparing himself to look once again into Rhyse's face.

Clint was too busy to notice much of this, however. As soon as he'd set himself down onto the ground, he pulled out two of the shotgun shells from his pocket and started digging out their contents with a small pocketknife. He made one pile of lead pellets and another pile of black powder. The rest of the packing went into a small hole he'd dug in the moist earth.

"What's all that for?" Joseph asked.

Clint scraped together all the gunpowder he'd collected in one hand, carefully gathering it all and pouring it into one of the empty shells. "Preparing for a little spell of my own."

• • •

It was closing in on noon when Joseph caught the first glimpse of the worn little dock on the edge of Zeller's property. Crouching low, he motioned for Clint and Monique to stop where they were and not make a sound. He scanned the area for any sign of Rhyse and the others, even though he was certain there wouldn't be any until it was too late to do anything about it.

Apparently, judging by the fewer guards walking around the place, Zeller thought that the demons only came out at night. Rhyse preferred it that way, but Joseph knew he certainly wouldn't pass up an opening like this just for effect. Between the dense swamp and the dock, there was only one guard. Joseph kept his head down and went back to tell Clint what he'd seen.

On his way to the property line, Clint thought back to the last time he'd been here and looked around for any trace of Eclipse. He figured the Darley Arabian might have broken loose and was waiting somewhere for a familiar face. It was also possible that Rhyse had done something to the stallion when Clint had been unconscious.

No, if Rhyse had done something to Eclipse, Clint was sure he would have heard about it from the man himself. That horse was around here somewhere. He could feel it.

Clint had walked about ten feet before one of the patrolling guns came running toward him.

"Hey, you there!" the guard shouted. "What are you doin' here?" The kid looked to be in his late teens and carried a Scofield rifle like it had been his last birthday present. His body was rail-thin and his face was scared. "State yer business, mister."

Raising his hands, Clint stopped in his tracks. "I'm not with Rhyse, so you can point that rifle somewhere else."

The kid stared at Clint for a second before his eyes darted to Monique, who was just now emerging from the bush. "Is that you, Miss Monique?"

"Yes, John," Monique said when she got to Clint's side. "Put the gun down and go get your father." After the kid took off toward the house, Monique turned to Clint and whispered, "Joseph stayed behind in case someone here recognized him."

"Good thinking. I only hope Rhyse doesn't find him first."

In a matter of seconds, a stocky man dressed in a white suit and a new Stetson emerged from the house. He was flanked by two armed guards, one of whom was the boy who had come out to greet them. Behind him was another man in his late twenties who looked almost like a younger duplicate of the man in the suit.

"That's James Zeller," Monique explained. "Behind him is his son Aubrey. That's the one Rhyse is after."

By now, Zeller was standing close enough for Clint to smell the lilac water on him. The stout Southerner took off his hat and wiped the sweat from his bald pate with a linen handkerchief. "Monique, what are you doin' with this one here?" he asked.

"Mister Zeller, this is Clint Adams and we want to help get rid of Mason Rhyse once and for all."

"Clint Adams? I think I heard'a you. You're a gunman, ain't you? Pretty famous from what I hear."

"That's not exactly the kind of fame I'm proud of, but it does seem to follow me," Clint said. "How long has Rhyse been coming after your boy?"

"We got word about a month back. Came as a note nailed to my home sayin' that if I didn't pay him five thousand dollars, Rhyse was gonna come in and take Aubrey."

"I take it you didn't pay?"

"Hell no! I don't hand out my money to any piece of trash that comes around askin' for it. Besides, I heard all the stories about Rhyse, especially when them fellas went missing awhile back and I'll be damned if I deal with a . . . thing like that preacher."

Clint spotted something moving along the furthest reaches of his peripheral vision. For a second, he thought it was Joseph, but when he turned to look, all he caught was a fleeting glimpse of black skin fading into the trees. "Rhyse is still coming for your son. Actually, he's here."

"What?!"

"Just tell your boys to follow my lead and not to do anything stupid. When this many nervous people with guns get together, blood usually follows."

Clint's words still hung in the air when a lanky figure seemed to materialize from the swamp. Even in broad daylight, Rhyse managed to make himself look like a demon spit up from the shadows. Walking next to him was Stokes, his face caked in a thick layer of dark mud that resembled his own flesh peeling off and dropping from his skull.

The pair walked out of the swamp and stood ominously in front of the group. Guards came running from every part of the property, readying their guns and looking toward the oldest Zeller for their orders. The man in the white suit kept his calm and fished a cigar from inside his jacket.

"You're the gunfighter here," Zeller said. "I'll let you take the lead."

Rhyse surveyed the group, which consisted of Clint, Monique, Zeller and three armed guards. He spotted Aubrey Zeller just before the young man dashed inside the house. Turning to Stokes, Rhyse whispered, "Why don't you find some cover and get ready to pick them off. Wait for my signal before you start shooting, though."

Stokes gripped the rifle he'd taken off the body of one of the other guards who'd fallen asleep at his post. It was an old man who'd carried that rifle and he was unlucky enough to spot Stokes when he'd been scouting earlier in the day. The rifle felt good in Stokes's hands and he nodded at Rhyse to let him know he would be covering his back.

"Why not just pay me now, Zeller?" Rhyse shouted. "It would save you and all these boys a lot of trouble. Might even keep some of them alive for a few more days."

Clint stepped forward, putting himself between Zeller and Rhyse. "You're a fraud, Rhyse. You tried your tricks on me and they didn't work. I'm still here and I'm not something you brought back from the dead. How long do you think you can live off of other people's fear? It doesn't look like you can make much off of those offerings, anyway. I mean, how is all of this trouble worth it to you? What do you expect to gain from everything you've been doing?"

"What do I gain?" Rhyse asked while pulling his gun and thumbing back the hammer. "What do I gain?" He took aim at Clint's head and walked closer, his finger tensing on the trigger.

Clint pulled his gun and was ready to fire before Rhyse took his next step. He sent a round straight into Rhyse's chest, dropping the preacher to the ground. He stood there waiting for Stokes to make his move when something else happened that he didn't expect.

Rhyse twitched. His legs jerked a bit and then he climbed back to his feet while looking down at the fresh hole in his coat. "What I gain . . . is immortality."

THIRTY-FOUR

Clint thought for sure that he'd hit Rhyse square in the chest. Just to be positive of that fact, he took aim and waited for the preacher to make his next move. Sure enough, Rhyse staggered around with a crazy smile on his face and pointed his gun back at Clint. Before the other man's pistol was fully raised, Clint fired and once again blasted Rhyse from his feet.

"You see," Rhyse screamed after he'd landed on his back. "You don't have strong enough magic to kill me!" This time, Rhyse propped himself up so that he was sitting with his hands supporting him from behind. "I'm gonna give Zeller and his men one chance to prove themselves to me before I smite everyone like the sinners they are. Kill them for me," he said, pointing to Clint and Monique. "Kill them and you will have my blessing. Do nothing and you will die by my hand."

For a few moments, there was no sound besides the constant chirping from the swamps and the echoing remnants of Rhyse's command. Then, Clint heard feet shifting in small, shuffling steps. Turning to look around him, he saw Zeller backing slowly away while his men grudgingly brandished their weapons, pointing them toward him.

"Don't be fooled by this con man!" Clint shouted to everyone in the area. "He's not a priest, a witch doctor, a demon or anything else but a pathetic little man who's not even good enough with a gun to do his own fighting. He tried to put me under his control, but it didn't work because I wasn't ready to believe in him."

The guards had stopped, not wanting to get too close to Clint. Also, they were listening to what he had to say. Keeping his eyes on Monique, James Zeller snapped his fingers and waved aside his men. They backed off, but still kept their guns pointed at Clint and ready to fire.

James was about to speak, but was interrupted by Rhyse's near-frantic voice.

"This can all stop right now, Zeller," Rhyse said. "Just have someone gun that man down and you can even keep your precious witch alive."

Clint, still staring Rhyse in the face, could see cracks forming in the madman's facade. "Why go through all this trouble for Zeller's son? Why not just move on like you always do and pick someone else to terrorize?"

"I am death," Rhyse said in a voice that could barely be heard. "I don't need a reason." And with a flick of his hand, he signaled toward the swamps behind him before dropping down to flatten himself against the ground.

A rifle shot cracked through the air and Clint could feel the stinging heat of a bullet whipping through the air, chewing a piece out of his cheek as it passed. He reflexively dropped to the ground and brought his hand up to feel a warm, wet patch of fresh blood on his face. The bullet had grazed him just below the scar on his cheek, but wasn't much more than a scratch.

After firing a shot toward the spot he'd seen Stokes head for, Clint sprung to his feet and grabbed hold of Monique, taking both of them down to the ground as another bullet passed over him with a sharp hiss.

For a second which seemed to freeze everything else around them, Clint and Rhyse locked stares as they both pressed themselves low to the packed mud. That was more than enough time for Clint to read the man's face and the glint in his eyes. It was plenty of time for him to realize just how crazy Rhyse truly was. He knew then that the false preacher truly wasn't ruled by rhyme or reason.

Whatever Rhyse did only made sense to himself and those that bought into the insane ramblings he constantly spewed from that mouth of his. Even the most cold-blooded of killers or sneakiest robbers were ruled by a certain set of rules and had a goal that could be understood.

Rhyse didn't care about money. All he wanted was the twisted kind of respect he got from people being scared of him. Looking into his eyes for that single second, Clint could tell what Rhyse was after.

Chaos.

And he'd already gotten it.

Suddenly, the world exploded around him as Clint looked away from Rhyse's insane face and turned his attention back to the gunfire that was erupting around him. Stokes was still taking the occasional shot, but now Zeller's men were beginning to return fire. A few of them were still standing there, looking at Clint and Monique as if trying to make their decision. Those were the ones that worried Clint more than the men that had already picked their side.

"You've got to get away from all of this," Clint said to Monique as they got their feet beneath them. "Rhyse is insane and who knows what the hell he wants here, but I know you'll get hurt if you don't get moving."

They were running in a low crouch toward the house with Clint's body shielding Monique's as the two remaining men who hadn't opened fire did just that. Another set of bullets cut through the air over Monique's and Clint's heads, buzzing around them like angry hornets. They ran around the building to find Joseph waiting there with his pistol drawn.

"Find somewhere safe and wait for the shooting to stop," Clint said to Monique as he took a small pouch from his belt. "Take this." Handing over the pouch, Clint explained the plan he'd been working on during their hike through the swamp. Monique took it all in and nodded as he told her a few things he needed her to find while everyone was distracted in front of the house.

"I'll do what I can," she agreed. "I think I know where to find what you need in their stables. Last time I was here, I saw they kept old wagons and a broken-down stove in there. That might do."

"It'll have to. Now get moving."

Clint could hear Rhyse starting to rant about something or another, but didn't even bother trying to make out the preacher's words. Instead, he looked at Joseph and held his pistol out in front of him. "Do you think you can find the man shooting from the trees?"

"That'd be Stokes," Joseph said with a nod. "I seen him work this way a few times and I can probably smoke him out."

"Good, because that's all I want you to do. Don't try to take him down, just get him to show himself. I'll take care of the rest."

Joseph hurried off toward the old dock. He hooked around behind the house and then curved back toward the bayou so that nobody in front of the estate would see where he was going. Clint watched him until he was nearly out of sight before turning his attention back toward the other direction.

The shots had stopped. He could hear a few confused voices talking amongst themselves, but those were nearly drowned out by Rhyse and his babbling. The preacher wasn't making any sense at all. There wasn't even a complete thought in the nonsense he was spouting. Clint shook his head and walked around the corner.

THIRTY-FIVE

As soon as Clint rounded the corner, he looked over to where Zeller and his boys had been standing. James was on the porch, crouched down behind a wooden railing that came down to form a small fence around most of the house. There were a few bullet holes in the thin wood, but his suit was still white and free of blood.

One of the boys with the rifles was slumped on the small set of steps leading to the porch, clutching at a wound in his side. Another stood out in the open in front of those steps, either to protect his fallen brother or too scared to move out of the line of fire. Two more guards had been running around the corner after Clint and when they saw him walking toward them, they stopped and started raising their guns in shaking hands.

Clint slowly dropped his gun back into its holster and held his hands out to the nervous young men with his palms facing out. "There's still plenty of time to change your minds about listening to that crazy man over there," he said while pointing to Rhyse, who stood in the same spot with his gun held loosely at his side.

"Shoot him!" Rhyse screamed. "Shoot him or I'll damn you all!"

Looking into the eyes of the men standing in front of him, Clint slowly shook his head. "You don't want to do this. Listen to his voice. He's crazy, pure and simple."

One of the guards, a dark-haired kid wearing a brown leather vest, nervously shifted on his feet. After a quick glance over his shoulder toward Rhyse, he lowered his rifle and ran to the porch steps to check on the wounded man lying there. The other guard was the one who had greeted Clint and Monique when they'd arrived and the expression on his face was one that Clint had seen many times on those who weren't used to the chaos of a gunfight.

Just as the boy was about to throw down his weapon, another shot came from the trees and clipped the kid through the neck. Out of sheer panic, the boy raised his rifle and fired, kicking up a mound of dirt to Clint's left. Running on nothing but blind panic, he levered in another round and swung the rifle to get a better shot at the man who wasn't more than seven feet away from him.

Clint didn't want to shoot the kid, but he also didn't want to bet his life on the guard missing a shot at almost point-blank range. Deciding on his action in less than a second, he sent himself into a motion that was almost too quick for anyone to see.

In the twitch of a muscle, Clint drew and fired. His bullet hit its mark and blew a hole through the nerves in the guard's shoulder, making it impossible for the kid to hold his rifle up any longer.

There was a sudden flash of pain in the boy's shoulder and then a wave of numbness washed through his entire side. The rifle slipped from his hands and hit the ground as the bullet's impact sent him reeling backwards and off his feet. He landed with a jarring thump that forced all the air from his lungs.

From the corner of his eye, Clint could see Rhyse moving toward the house. Turning to see what the preacher was doing, Clint swept his foot out and kicked the rifle beneath the stairs. "Get inside," he yelled to the people gathered on the porch. Before he could make sure the Zellers were out of harm's way, Clint saw the preacher barreling toward him with an insane fire in his eyes.

Just as he was about to turn toward the incoming maniac, Clint felt something crash against his ribs and realized that Rhyse had launched himself toward him and impacted with his shoulder. Clint twisted around while grabbing hold of Rhyse so that the preacher hit the ground first. The maneuver took every bit of strength Clint had, but it worked and they both toppled down as another shot rang out in the distance.

There was nothing left in Rhyse's face except rage. Having decided that the preacher was too far gone to figure out, Clint was forced to react to the crazy man instead of out-guess him. Rhyse was a flurry of fists and curses as he struggled to get out from under Clint while doing as much damage as he could in the process.

Clint felt blow after blow impact against his face and chest. They all came in twice as fast as he would have thought possible from someone of Rhyse's size. When one of the preacher's fists slammed against the bloody scratch on Clint's face, blood began to cover both of them, flowing from one man and dripping onto the other.

Another shot sounded from the trees, but it wasn't fired from the rifle and no bullet came toward the house. Clint heard the shot and figured it came from a pistol. The thought went through his mind automatically as his hands struggled to get ahold of Rhyse's flailing arms. Once he got the preacher pinned to the ground, Clint smashed his forehead against Rhyse's nose, hitting hard enough that he could hear the wet crunch of cartilage snapping on impact.

Rhyse seemed about ready to take another swing, but then his eyes clouded over and rolled back into his head as the pain from his shattered nose sunk its teeth fully into the preacher's nerves. His head lolled to the side before dropping back against the ground, where it stayed as the rest of his body went limp.

With his fist balled up and ready to deliver another blow, Clint stayed where he was until he was sure Rhyse was unconscious. Then he got up and dusted himself off before turning around to check on the wounded guards in front of the house. Kneeling close to the porch steps, Clint reached out to check on the bloody young men.

"You'll be all right," he said to the kid who'd been shot through the side. "But we need to get you to a doctor right away." Then he looked at the guard he'd shot.

The boy's arm was covered in blood, but was already starting to move again as the shock from getting shot was dying down in his system. "Sorry I had to do that, kid," Clint said. "But I needed—"

"You don't have to explain," the boy replied. "It's me that should be apologizing. I don't know why, but I . . . I just wanted that devil man to go away, an' since I couldn't shoot him, I . . ." He turned his face away, ashamed. "I'm sorry."

"What the hell was all that!?" James Zeller blustered as he stomped down the steps to crouch down next to his sons. "I ain't never seen anything like that. He's got to be dead, but he just kept comin'!"

Clint stepped back to let the others pick up the wounded boys and carry them inside. James stood by to let the younger men do all the lifting, while looking down at Rhyse and shaking his head in confused wonder. Stooping down to Rhyse's sleeping form, Clint pulled open the skinny preacher's shirt.

"There's your miracle," Clint said with a wave of his hand.

"I'll be damned," Zeller whispered as he tapped his foot against the steel plate that was strapped to Rhyse's chest by a pair of thick ropes.

The rusted piece of metal looked as though it had been roughly cut from the side of a steam engine and was dented in several spots, which looked as if they had been poked by someone's finger. The rust had been freshly chipped off in two places where Clint's bullets had found their marks.

Clint looked back toward the line of trees and spotted a figure emerging from the bayou. Walking with a slight limp and gripping his right leg, Joseph staggered into the open a few steps before falling over. Clint rushed over to him and helped him back to his feet.

"We need to get you inside before the other one shows up," Clint said.

Joseph grunted as he tried to put some of his weight on the bad leg. "What other one?"

"There were two other men with Rhyse. The black man and the other tall one who must be hiding somewhere around here."

They were halfway to the house when Joseph said, "Lovario's dead. And Stokes got away."

"I heard gunshots out there. Did you get him before he did this to you?"

"I . . . I don't know. As soon as he saw you get the drop on Rhyse, Stokes took off. I tried to follow, but he put a round through my damn leg."

"We don't have time to worry about that," Clint said. "We've got injured men to tend to and one to hand over to the law."

Just then, Clint saw something that made the entire trip back worthwhile. Coming from behind the house, looking nervously from side to side, was Monique and she wasn't alone.

"Is it safe?" she asked while looking at Rhyse and then toward the trees.

"For now," Clint said while walking toward her and the horse she was leading. Stroking Eclipse's muzzle, Clint felt better with each anxious whinny that came from the Darley Arabian's mouth. "Did you find the other things I asked for?"

Monique nodded while looking over to Rhyse. "Yes, but it looks like we might not need it."

"Normally, I'd say you were right, but with this one . . . I'm not taking any more chances."

THIRTY-SIX

James Zeller sent his youngest boy into town to fetch the sheriff. In the meantime, everyone who was able came out to the porch to help the two wounded young men inside. Clint and Joseph took the job of making sure Rhyse was tied up with enough knots to keep the skinny demon from being able to move so much as a little finger. Once that was done, Clint found James Zeller standing inside the front room of the estate.

"Mister Zeller," Clint said.

The squat little man in white turned and immediately extended a hand out to Clint. "I want to thank you, sir," he said. "Thank you for saving my boy from that madman outside. I only wish you would've finished him off instead of just wounding the son of a bitch."

"Well, we need to do a few things before we get rid of Rhyse for good. Before that, however, I wanted to thank you for keeping my horse for me."

Zeller nodded. "Ah yes. That's a fine animal. I don't suppose you'd let me take him off your hands? I'd be willing to pay handsomely."

"Not on your life."

"I figured as much. I also knew you'd be coming back for him, but I wasn't sure if you'd make it through the swamps and past those guns that Rhyse had workin' for him."

Clint thought back to his trip through the bayou and the things that had almost eaten him and everyone else alive.

"There were a few close calls, but we managed."

Zeller puffed on a cigar and led Clint further inside the house where Monique was tending to the wounded men. "You ask me, I'd tell you the man's just cracked," he said while tapping his head with a pudgy finger. "Up here, you know?"

"Yeah, I think I figured that one out the hard way."

"You know how much he asked me for as a tribute? Three dollars and six cents. Every town for miles around have been talkin' about that crazy man who lives in the swamps. Up to now, he'd been harmless. Just toss him some food or a few coins and he went on his way. Those people that went missin', most everyone figured they'd gotten lost in the swamps or just picked up and left."

"Well, I've got something in mind to take care of this crazy man from the swamps," Clint said. "Because once Rhyse is gone, some other freak will move in and take his place. There's always plenty of violent men looking for a reputation and if they can't get their own, they'll try to take over Rhyse's."

"So what do you propose?"

"I'm going to make sure no one will want to follow in Rhyse's footsteps."

The sheriff of Jespin was a man named Brody and he came back with the Zeller boy about an hour later. Brody stood as tall as Clint, but with a more muscular build. He wore a double-rig holster and walked with the speed of a man confident that everything else in the world would slow down and wait for him.

The sheriff walked up to Clint after James pointed him in the right direction. "Mister Zeller tells me you caught the man that's been threatening his boy," Brody said in a deep, resonating voice.

Clint hooked a thumb toward the barn where Eclipse had been kept. "Right this way, Sheriff."

Rhyse was trussed up like a calf at a county fair and he still hadn't moved since the last time Clint had checked on him. The skinny man looked like a collection of pieced-together skin and grizzled old bones. His clothes even seemed to have deflated without the preacher's hot air to fill them up.

"So this is the legend of the swamps, huh?" Brody asked. "Doesn't look like much to me."

"Sure, not after he's been knocked cold and tied up. If you thought so little of this man, why didn't you ever go after him?"

"Because I'm not in the business of chasing down ghost stories."

"Even when those ghost stories threaten to kidnap one of your townspeople's sons?"

Brody sighed and looked around to make sure that they were the only ones in the barn besides the unconscious prisoner. "It's Adams, right?"

Clint nodded.

"The people round here have blamed this man for everything from floods to things they lost in their yards. I've heard plenty about you and I know you've helped a lot of lawmen in your time. You put yourself in my place and tell me that you would've chased down every rumor of this old coot that's been circulatin' for the last few years."

Clint couldn't really argue with that one. Looking down at Rhyse, he noticed the man had begun to stir. Leading the sheriff outside, Clint went over a few things he'd been wanting to ask and found Brody to be very receptive to what he wanted to do. Finally, Clint helped drag Rhyse away from the barn and loaded him onto Eclipse's back.

"Untie me now," Rhyse demanded in an angry, if a little slurred voice. "Set me free or I'll give you nightmares that you've never—"

"Shut up before I knock your brains around some more," Clint snarled. "It's all over for you. Everyone knows about your little trick with the metal plate and soon I'll be starting some stories of my own."

"What do you mean?"

"Stories about how your resurrections aren't anything more than throwing some dirt over a man and then helping him dig his way out again." Clint looked for any sign that his words were having an effect on Rhyse.

He'd gotten better reactions when talking to Eclipse.

Since Clint wasn't in the habit of talking to walls, he decided to swear off talking to Rhyse as well. The ride to the sheriff's office was short, but not short enough. By the time he pulled Eclipse to a stop in front of the small building, he was ready to toss the old man out of the saddle and into the mud. One of Brody's deputies, a large man in his early twenties who wore his shirtsleeves rolled up over tree trunks disguised as forearms, came outside just in time to catch Rhyse around the shoulders.

"Brody's on the way back," Clint said. "He'll know what to do with that one."

The deputy looked confused, but didn't try to stop Clint as he rode Eclipse back to the Zeller estate. Monique was waiting outside for him, wiping her hands dry on a linen cloth. Joseph stood nearby and jumped to his feet when Clint rode up to the porch.

"I'm surprised you're still around," Clint said to Joseph. "Your horse can't be tied up too far from here."

"She's still in the swamp. I can get to her easy enough, but I wanted to see you first. You know, to make sure that I couldn't do anything else to help."

"Actually," Clint said. "I'm glad you brought that up. The first thing I need is some of that war paint Rhyse made you put on your face. Then come find me after dark. You've got to play dead one more time."

THIRTY-SEVEN

Joseph walked with Clint and Monique so they could decide how they would spend their last night in Jespin, Louisiana. With that done, Joseph headed off for the swamps to find his horse and Clint headed into town to find a place where he could relax for a while. Jespin wasn't exactly famous for its entertainment, but it did have a saloon which was all Clint was looking for.

He got a sour beer from the barkeep and sat himself down into a straight-backed chair in the middle of a dark room that felt hotter than the swamp and smelled just as bad. Sipping the foul brew, Clint closed his eyes, took a breath and felt the knots in his shoulders begin to loosen. Monique took a beer as well and when she took a sip, she smiled widely.

"This is the first time I've ever tried the beer here," she pointed out.

"Yeah?"

"It's really bad. Tastes like they sucked it out from the bottom of a pond."

"Yeah."

Both of their mugs were already drained and they sat there for a few minutes, just enjoying the silence that had fallen between them. Finally, Clint asked, "Want another?"

Monique handed over her mug and flashed him a warm smile. "Yeah."

• • •

The saloon had a pair of rooms for rent on its second floor. Clint rented out one of them and even paid the extra fifty cents to get himself a bath. Sitting in the large metal tub, he soaped himself down twice before the stink of the bayou came off his skin. There was a knock on the door just as Clint had put his head on the edge of the tub and was about to doze off.

Hoping it was the barkeep's wife with another pitcher of hot water, he pulled a towel over himself and said, "Come in."

Instead of the chunky redhead who'd given him the key to his room, it was Monique who opened the door. To make things better, she even had a pitcher of hot water in her hands.

"Sara gave me this," she said as she walked in and locked the door behind her. "She told me you might be getting cold right about now."

Monique set the pitcher on a small table near the door and reached up to loosen the strings that laced across the front of her dress. The material was pushed apart by her rounded breasts and began to slide down off her shoulders. Her dark, creamy skin shimmered in the sunlight that filtered in through the room's only window. Clint could see by the way the dress clung to her body that she wore nothing underneath it.

She brought the pitcher over to the tub, walked behind Clint and started to slowly pour the steaming water over his shoulders and onto his chest. Clint felt as though his entire body was going to melt in the luxurious heat.

As the water continued to trickle down his body, Monique reached out to run her hands along Clint's skin. Her fingers massaged his naked skin and worked their way down until the pitcher was empty and the gentle little rain had come to a stop.

"Looks nice in there," she said as she tugged her dress down until it was gathered at her waist. "Mind if I join you?"

"I'd mind more if you didn't join me," Clint replied while pulling the dress down over her hips.

Monique wriggled free of the clothing until it dropped around her ankles. Stepping out of the dress, she grabbed hold of the side of the tub and stepped into the hot water. With the balmy heat that was already in the air, the water felt like a soft cushion against her entire body. Crouching down to cup her hands together and fill them with water, she brought the liquid up to her neck and let it flow over her dark, supple breasts.

Clint watched as she got herself nice and wet for him. The water splashed down her stomach and ran between her legs, making the little patch of hair slick and shiny. The way she was squatting, with her legs spread just right, he could see the thin lips between her thighs blushing as the water ran over them and trickled into the tub.

Taking another handful of water, Monique splashed some in her hair before lowering herself into the bath and leaning against the side opposite of Clint. Her feet slid over his legs, playfully rubbing his thigh and then brushing up against his growing hardness. Monique then inched forward with her hands feeling in his lap until they gripped his shaft and started stroking it slowly and smoothly.

Unable to hold himself back, Clint moved his hands beneath the water, snaking them around her back and then running down along her sides. He enjoyed the feel of her full, rounded hips as they squirmed between his palms. Her legs were strong with knotted muscles and wrapped around him to pull herself closer to him.

"Most men look at me," she said, "but they never touch me. I think they're afraid I might curse them or something silly like that."

Clint's hands cupped her buttocks and pulled her tight against him. His rigid cock pushed between her legs and he slipped inside of her with a gentle shift of his hips. "Don't you do curses?"

"Yes," she laughed as her eyes shut and her head arched back with the waves of pleasure coursing through her body. "But they only work when people believe in them. And besides, I work more as a healer." Moving her hips in a slow circle, Monique rubbed her body against his until his shaft was rubbing perfectly against her most sensitive spots.

Clint moved forward now with Monique held tight in his arms. "You're doing a wonderful job, then, because I'm feeling much better." He pressed Monique up against the side of the tub and cupped her from behind. With her hips raised slightly, he was able to kneel in the water and slide in and out of her until they created waves that started sloshing onto the floor.

Monique leaned forward, holding on to Clint's neck and wrapping her legs around him as he stood up and carried her over to the bed. Climbing out of the tub, he caught one of his feet on the edge and stumbled forward until they landed on the thin mattress with him on top of her. They laughed for a few seconds, feeling easy in each other's company. That laughter faded quickly, however, as Clint looked down to see her beautiful ebony body covered in beads of water roaming freely over her flesh.

Clint leaned forward to run his mouth over Monique's skin. He started at the wetness between her legs, darting his tongue in and out of her as she bucked her hips against his face. Then he moved his way up over her stomach and between her breasts. When he began nibbling on her neck, he reached up to run his palms over her nipples, feeling them grow harder with every stroke.

"Oh, Clint, don't make me wait anymore," Monique pleaded urgently.

Before he could move another muscle, she reached down to wrap her hand around his thick shaft and guide it between her legs. When he plunged deeply inside, she gasped and clawed at his back while biting down on her lower lip. Monique's legs were squeezing him tight, massaging his sides as Clint thrust with his entire body until it felt like the entire bed was rocking back and forth.

"That's it, baby," she whispered. "I like it right there." One of her legs hooked up and around Clint's back to pull him in even closer. The other leg went over Clint's shoulder, which positioned her body so that his hard cock penetrated so deeply that her eyes shot open and a little squeal came from the back of her throat.

Clint slid his hand over the leg on his shoulder, feeling the taut muscles in her calf and the ones straining in her thigh. Moving down to grip her buttocks, he savored the smooth solidity of them as they clenched every time he thrust inside of her. Her pussy was tight and wet around his member and when he gave her bottom a little slap, she squealed even louder.

Suddenly, Monique put her hands on Clint's hips and pushed him away. She looked at him with lust smoldering in her eyes, crawled off the bed and stood to lean down so she could grab hold of the mattress with her rounded butt raised in the air.

Moving around so that he was standing behind her, Clint
reached down to slip a finger into the moist warm lips she was
offering him. Monique groaned as his fingers slid inside of
her, pressing her chest down even harder onto the bed so she
could push her bottom up a little higher as an invitation.

Clint was more than happy to take her up on her offer and
worked his pole between her thighs and grabbed hold of her
hips. He thrust into her hard and deep, just the way she'd been
begging for it. Every time his hips pushed against her tight
rump, she gripped the blankets and pulled them around her
face so she could cry into them as loudly as she wanted.

Soon, her back was glistening with sweat and when Clint
thrust into her for the last time, both of their cries filled the
room.

THIRTY-EIGHT

Stokes waited in the bayou until night had fallen over the swamps. He was sitting at the old campsite near the river, resting on the same fallen log where Rhyse had gone over his plan to raid the Zeller estate. It felt like that had happened so long ago when it had actually only been a little over a day. The tall black man hunched over as he sat and watched the water turn from dark green to black. Before he knew it, the stars were flickering overhead like tiny porch lights in the distance.

His momma always told him those stars were lights sent out from all the souls in heaven that needed to light up the sky so the ones left on earth would never get lost. Stokes hadn't thought about his momma for a long time, since Rhyse never liked to hear about anything that happened before the resurrection. Now, with Rhyse in a Jespin jail cell, Stokes had some time to think for himself.

He thought about all the strange things he'd seen in Rhyse's company and all the strange things he'd done himself. Sometimes he thought Rhyse wasn't really an angel. Sometimes, he thought he hadn't been brought back to life.

Sitting there, Stokes felt as though his mind was starting to play tricks on him. He could still hear Rhyse's sermons. If that man really was an angel, what would happen to someone who crossed him? Especially now, in his time of greatest need?

Stokes had his doubts, but he'd seen too much to be sure

that those doubts could be trusted. If he was wrong, if Rhyse really was the angel of death, then Stokes knew his soul would fry in the lowest pit in hell as a punishment for a trespass like the one he was considering.

Suddenly, Stokes felt as though he could hear Rhyse's voice shaking him out of his train of thought. Reaching down to the small wooden bowl at his feet, he busied himself preparing the black paste that would cover his skin when he headed back into Jespin.

It was senseless to sit around and think about what his life had been like before. Almost as stupid as it was for a man to waste his days thinking back to his childhood. Stokes knew he had a lot more waiting for him when he'd completed his work for Rhyse. Someday, he would be allowed to move on and answer the beckoning he saw in the sky.

Of course Rhyse was an angel. The way he saw it, Stokes would only be throwing away the future of his eternal soul to think otherwise.

He dipped his finger into the warm, sticky mud and smeared the mixture onto his face. Trying not to think about the things he would have to do to win Rhyse's freedom, Stokes instead focused on the torments he would be avoiding later on.

"They can't kill me," he whispered to himself as he thought about the men with guns guarding Rhyse. "They can't kill me, so there ain't nothin' to be scared of."

Once the paste was applied and his skin smelled like the bayou floor, Stokes checked the rifle to make sure it was loaded. He had plenty of spare shells and knew the shortest way to get to the town's jail. All he had to do was shoot the man with the keys to Rhyse's cell and the preacher would take care of the rest.

Stokes swung himself up into the saddle of his horse. It felt good to be riding again after all the skulking around he'd been doing. Sitting up high on the back of the animal made him feel like he did when Lovario had been alive. Stokes felt larger than life. More than that . . . he felt he was beyond life.

A low chant started in the big man's chest, sounding like his soul was resonating inside of him. It grew until his throat tensed and the song spilled out to swirl around him, just as it had when he was in church. Thinking of church made him think of the bloody priest's collar that Rhyse wore, which was an image that always spooked Stokes something fierce.

With the fear came strength and with the strength came the cold that locked his eyes so they were looking straight ahead, unable to see anything but what he'd convinced himself that he needed to see. It was that expression that Rhyse liked to see. When he wore it, Stokes was ready to act his role as an undead soldier.

He felt the second identity settle over him like an unwelcome cowl that had been thrown over his head by a kidnapper who'd taken him out of his bed. He would have thrown it off, but Stokes knew that to do so meant throwing away his chances of ever seeing his family again. At least that had been what Rhyse had said and until he found out otherwise, Stokes would do what he needed to do.

Leaning down in the saddle, he tugged at the reins of the other horses until they came loose from where they'd been tied. Lovario's was given a smack on the rump and allowed to run free. Stokes took hold of Rhyse's horse and wrapped its reins around his own saddle horn so he could lead it back to town. There was supposed to be a third horse there that had belonged to Joseph Terray, but it wasn't anywhere to be found. Stokes figured the traitor had come back for it sometime earlier in the day and on some level, the black man hoped Joseph had taken his horse and ridden far away.

Joseph seemed like a good enough sort and Stokes knew Rhyse would want him dead for choosing to pick sides against him. Thinking back to the look on Joseph's face when Miss Monique had worked her spell on him, Stokes wondered if she could see her way to free his soul as well.

Then, just as the possibility entered his brain, Stokes swore he could hear Rhyse hissing into his ear. "She's a witch. A witch!"

Once again, the coldness settled over the black man's eyes and he clenched his jaw tight enough to crack the thick layer of mud on his face. His fate was sealed. It was too late to be saved. The devil had too firm a grip on his soul.

Snapping his reins, Stokes urged his horse into the swamps. Jespin wasn't far away, but he would take his time getting there. After all . . . he needed the time to prepare his soul for the havoc he needed to wreak.

THIRTY-NINE

As darkness came to the swamps, Clint was busy making his preparations. He'd assembled the pieces he needed and had spent some time talking with Monique about exactly what all the legends were that had been built around Rhyse and his men. Clint then got together with Joseph, who had done his best to copy the mixture that had been used to paint their faces on the few times he'd been on raids with the "undead."

It was pitch black before Clint was done with his tasks, but he didn't want to work too quickly. His hands worked expertly as they cleaned out two more shotgun shells and re-packed them. Snapping the sawed-off weapon closed, he almost tucked the gun away, but stopped and double-checked that the ammo inside was the ammo he'd prepared. After all, his plan didn't call for anyone to be killed.

Especially not him.

Joseph walked around to the back of the livery where Clint was working. Eclipse shifted in his stall, as if reacting to the ghostly visage that had appeared in the moonlight. Looking up from his preparations, Clint nodded to the man who looked more like a decaying monster.

"You ready?" Clint asked.

"As ready as I'll ever be. I'll be honest, though, I'd rather not have this stuff on my face again."

"Don't worry. After tonight, I'm hoping that nobody will be wearing that stuff around here again."

"Are you sure Stokes will be coming tonight?"

Clint made sure the shotgun wasn't cocked before fitting it beneath his gun belt at the small of his back. "The way I see it, if he doesn't come back tonight, that means he's decided to run off on his own. And without Rhyse, there isn't much of a gang left. Are you sure that body you found in the swamp was Lovario?"

Joseph shuddered at the very memory of what he'd found earlier in the day when he went for his horse. He'd been searching for Stokes when he stumbled upon the grizzly remains. "Yeah. I'm sure."

"Then this Stokes is the only one left and without a leader, I don't think he'll do much of anything besides hide. If that's the case, then that solves our problem."

There was a minute of silence as Clint stood and checked his pistol, making sure every chamber was filled and that all the metal was clean and oiled.

"But you don't think that will happen, do you?" Joseph asked.

Clint holstered his gun and walked over to an empty stall that he'd been using as a kind of workshop. On the ground was a square metal door from an old pot-bellied stove that Monique had borrowed from the Zellers. He picked up a small pouch filled with the gunpowder from the shotgun shells he'd taken apart and crouched over the piece of black rusted metal. Using the little door like a plate, Clint smeared some glue onto the door and then emptied the gunpowder over it.

Finally, Clint answered Joseph's question. "Honestly, I wish that Stokes would just ride away and put all this craziness behind him. But I saw the look in his eyes. He follows Rhyse blindly out of loyalty and fear. If I put myself in that man's place, I'd want to come in and try to break Rhyse out of that cell as soon as I could."

"But he's only one man. How could he stand up against Sheriff Brody and his deputies?"

"There were only three of you and Rhyse managed to get entire towns to back down. Besides, these people are still afraid of the stories surrounding Rhyse and his followers. I've seen firsthand how a bunch of scared people can turn the tide in a fight. The sheriff might stand his ground, but it won't matter if he gets outnumbered by his own townspeople with guns in their hands."

"So Stokes dies and Rhyse rots in jail? That hardly seems fair."

Patting the black crust that he'd created on top of the oven door, Clint made sure the gunpowder was thick in the middle and wasn't about to blow off when the metal plate was moved. "Monique has heard all the stories and knows just about everything that Rhyse's gang has done. Rhyse did all the killing himself."

Joseph nodded. "Far as I could tell, that Stokes was a helluva scout and tracker. He was strong as an ox and scary as the devil, but I never seen him kill."

"Exactly. He's not a killer and neither am I. That's why I want to keep him alive if at all possible and if that means going through a little extra work, then that's what I'll do."

Joseph started laughing. The sound seemed funny in itself coming from a man resembling death warmed over. "Maybe I'm a little too tired, but that just seems funny. We're going through all this so we can keep alive a man who thinks he's already dead. That's a good one."

Clint smiled and shook his head. The expression he wore, however, was not that of a man who found any of this funny. "Go ahead and get all of that out of your system. But just because Stokes hasn't killed anyone yet, don't think that means we're all safe."

That took the joy right out of Joseph's voice. He quickly pulled himself together and rubbed at his eyes. "I'm sorry, you're right."

Turning his attention back to what he was doing, Clint picked up the metal grate and walked out of the stall. "Let's just get going and try to do all this right. Now, why don't you go over the plan one more time."

"We've been through this already."

"And we'll go through it again."

Sighing like a boy reluctant to go back to his studies, Joseph recited the details of Clint's plan while ticking off every step on his fingers. As he talked, Clint led him to a section of the street half a block away from the sheriff's office. It was there that Clint set the plate down and covered it with a thin layer of weeds he'd pulled up from the ground.

Joseph finished talking just as Clint straightened up and took a breath. He stared straight into Joseph's eyes, looking for any hint of possible trouble. As far as he could tell, the other man was nervous, but not too scared to complete his task.

"All right," Clint said as he spotted Monique coming out of the saloon. "We all know what to do, so let's get to it."

Joseph nodded, turned and headed off into a side street where he could keep an eye on the surrounding bayou and keep hidden in the shadows. Once there, he felt around in the darkness until he found the small tin cup he'd hidden there earlier. He dipped his fingers inside, scooped up a little of the thick paste he'd mixed up and touched it to the corners of his mouth where the stuff had flaked off from talking. Finished, he set the cup down on top of a small crate where it would be easy to find when it was needed again.

Monique walked up to Clint's side, holding her arms tight against her body. Even though the night was just as balmy as the day, she still felt cold. Only when Clint rubbed his hands along her arms did she feel slightly warm again.

"I still wish you'd just capture him like we did with Rhyse," she said. "I've got a bad feeling about all of this."

Clint could hear the sound of an approaching horse coming from the direction of the swamp. "All of this nonsense needs to stop. Rhyse is nothing but a crazy man who lives in the bayou, but people are afraid of him like he was some kind of devil. Nobody should be afraid of being stolen away from their own homes and after tonight, a lot of folks will be sleeping easier."

Looking up at him, Monique pressed herself against Clint's chest and then pulled away just as quickly. "Just be careful," she said softly.

"I will. Did you get what I wanted from Sheriff Brody?"

She reached into a pocket stitched to the side of her dress and removed something flat and square that was wrapped in a cloth stained with gun oil. When Monique handed it over, she seemed glad to have it out of her possession.

Clint unwrapped the bundle and removed the small copper flask belonging to Mason Rhyse. The dented container looked like it had gone through hell, which seemed oddly appropriate considering its owner.

"I checked out that whiskey just like you asked," Monique said. "And you were right. There's definitely something mixed in that smelled a little like Curare."

"Curare?"

"It's a poison that tribal hunters used to use to paralyze their prey. From what I could tell, there was enough in that whiskey to knock a man out for a good long while. One sip too many and someone could've been dead for real."

Clint could still taste the stuff on his lips from when it had been forced into his mouth. "Where would someone like Rhyse get a tropical poison?"

Monique shrugged. "My mother's got a jar of it in her parlor. It's rare, but not impossible to find. What are you going to do with it?"

"I'm not sure yet," Clint said with a scheming glint in his eye. "But I'll think of something."

FORTY

When Stokes rode out of the swamp, he parted the trees as though he was walking onto a stage. The horse beneath him was grateful for the exercise after having been tied up for too long and its breath came from its nostrils like steam from an engine. The tall black man was made up the way Rhyse had taught him and the few people who'd seen him enter the town limits looked at him with stark fear in their eyes.

Just like they were supposed to.

Jespin was not a town that stayed awake much past dark. But tonight, there was something in the air. Stokes couldn't quite pin it down, but he felt an energy that crackled on the wind and buzzed against his skin. His eyes scanned the street, moving in his head like cold white orbs in a field of coal.

His gun was slung in a harness on the side of his saddle and when he caught the first glimpse of Clint walking toward him, Stokes pulled the rifle and held it over his shoulder.

"You know what I'm here for," Stokes said. "So let Rhyse go and I'll be on my way. The longer you hold him, the madder he'll get."

"Oh, we sure don't want that," Clint replied sarcastically.

Stokes swung down off his horse and landed with both boots planted firmly in the mud. The rifle looked like a child's toy in his massive hand and he held it pointed at the ground as though he didn't even think he'd need it. "You had your chance to stand with us and you refused. I don't know how you broke free, but you did. So hand Rhyse over to me so we can move on and you can enjoy your life."

"Those aren't our only choices here, you know. You can leave this insanity behind and let Rhyse rot in his cell. There's nothing holding you here."

For a second, Stokes looked as though he was going to set his rifle down. But then the black man shook his head and stepped forward. "It ain't that easy," he said while raising his rifle.

Clint held his ground until he got a good look into the other man's eyes. He was looking for a glimmer of hope, just a little spark of reason in Stokes's face, but instead found nothing besides the painted mask that Rhyse had drawn on him. Apparently, all of Clint's preparations hadn't been wasted.

Taking a few steps back, Clint looked around to make sure of his position. He also checked to make sure that Sheriff Brody was doing his part by keeping any wandering towns-people out of the line of fire. The jail was only three buildings away and when he was halfway there, Clint stopped in front of an alley and waited.

"Stokes!"

The voice wasn't particularly menacing, but it was more than enough to grab the big man's attention. He already knew who was speaking and when Stokes turned to see Monique staring at him from the doorway of a darkened storefront, his eyes widened and his grip tightened around the rifle.

Monique hadn't known Stokes too well before he'd been kidnapped, but she'd seen the look in his eyes too many times in other people. It was the look of those who didn't know the difference between what she did and what the Haitian voodoo practitioners used to do in their blood ceremonies and sacrifice rituals. Rather than try to convince him otherwise, Monique let him think whatever he wanted. In fact, she put a little extra heat in her stare as she slowly walked into the street.

"You stay away from me, witch," Stokes warned as the rifle in his hand slowly tracked between Clint and Monique.

She didn't show the first sign of fear, but rather stood her ground once she was standing across from Clint. "I won't al-low you to hurt anyone here," she said. "Put your gun down and I can take away what Rhyse did to you."

Stokes's mind raced with the memory of what he'd seen her

do to Joseph. He remembered the look of awakened joy on the man's face and how even he could feel the weight that she'd lifted off of him. His rifle started to lower, but then Stokes shook his head and brought it up again. "No! He's too close. He'll know what you done an' he'll just make it worse on me."

Wanting to give the man one last chance, Clint stood with his empty hands held in front of him and spoke in a calm, reasonable tone. "Think about it, Stokes. Rhyse was fooling you. He was fooling everyone. You saw him bury me and I came out fine."

The black man seemed confused. He blinked his eyes as though there was smoke blowing in his face. "But . . . why would he do that? Why do all those things 'less it was true?"

"Because he's crazy," Clint answered. "It's as simple as that. You can't figure out a crazy man. He's just sick."

Stokes seemed to think that over for a second. Inside, he wrestled with what he wanted to believe and what he'd been programmed to believe. Just when it seemed he was going to make a decision, he would come up with another reason to change his mind.

Watching this, Clint waited until he realized that the other man simply wasn't going to be able to go back without a little help. In fact, he'd been counting on that when he'd pieced together his plan. Better to fix Stokes by using his beliefs, he figured, than to try to force him to go against them.

Turning subtly to look down the alley, Clint nodded when he was sure Stokes wasn't looking. A few seconds later, Joseph emerged from the alley with his back straight and his eyes cold and void of emotion. The paste on his skin caught the moonlight to give him the look of something freshly removed from the soil.

"He's right, Clint," Joseph said. "Rhyse is too strong." Turning to Stokes, he took a few steps toward the black man and pulled his gun. He then pointed the gun at Clint. "I was wrong to turn on the one who'd granted me my second life. And now, I only hope I can help free him to get back into his good graces."

Stokes didn't know what to make of this at all. First, he pointed the rifle at Joseph and then he turned it back on Clint. Before he could think too much about what had happened,

Clint started taking slow, backward steps toward the sheriff's office.

"Do you know why that one survived the resurrection?" Joseph asked Stokes. "It's because of her help." Pointing toward Monique, Joseph looked at her with the same wild eyes that marked Rhyse and all of his men. "She is a witch and her magic was strong enough to resurrect that man and keep him under her control. Even Rhyse fears her."

"B . . . but, I saw her fix you," Stokes stammered.

"What you saw was a lie that Rhyse wanted you to see," Clint said quickly. "But his lies are over! He was old and frail and when his time came, his magic flowed out of him like he sprang a leak"

Joseph turned to Clint with an angry fire in his eyes. "What are you saying?"

"I'm saying Rhyse is dead." Clint stared directly at Stokes. "At least the part of him that matters is. All that's left in that cell is a raving old man."

Furious, Joseph charged at Clint, screaming, "I don't believe you! Rhyse is the power over life itself!" When he got to Clint, Joseph swung his fist with every ounce of strength he had, connecting hard enough to send Clint staggering back a few steps.

Clint struck out with a fist to the other man's stomach, but Joseph had worked himself into a frenzy and easily dodged out of the way. When his fist hit nothing but open air, Clint found himself overextended, giving Joseph a free shot at his back.

Rather than slam another fist into Clint's body, Joseph plucked the shotgun from Clint's gun belt and pointed it at him.

Rubbing his jaw, Clint saw the gun pointed at him and took several steps back. "What're you going to do with that, Joseph? You should have shot me when you had the chance. I've got Rhyse's magic now and that's all that can give your life back to you. Now both of you belong to me."

Joseph shook his head and cocked back the hammers for the shotgun.

Watching all of this, Stokes didn't know whether he should help Joseph or take a shot at Clint. His decision was made for him when the shotgun exploded with a deafening roar and a plume of smoke filled the air in front of him. The sound was so loud that Stokes wasn't even able to hear as Clint dropped to the ground and crawled off for the alley. As soon as Clint pulled himself between the buildings, Joseph fired again.

Monique rushed forward and placed her hands on Clint's still form and began to cry. As Stokes's hearing cleared up, he could tell she wasn't crying tears of sorrow, but was wailing out a series of words that echoed down the street like a strange, melodious chant.

The big black man walked forward, but stopped when he saw that the witch woman was performing a ritual over the dead body. She held a small bag in her hands and when she shook the bag over the body, Clint moved. His arms pushed at the ground and eventually he got up to his knees. When he turned around, his face was covered with the same white paste as Joseph's.

FORTY-ONE

Stokes all but jumped backwards when he saw the woman perform her resurrection. Lifting the little bag high over her head, she got up and walked over to the storefront across the street. She then turned to Stokes and held the bag out to him.

"You know who I am," she stated. "You know who my mother is and you know that her power runs through me."

Stokes was too stunned by what he'd seen to talk. Instead, he simply nodded his head and shifted on his feet.

Monique spoke in the same monotone she used in all her chants. "That man had taken Rhyse's power, which let him come back from the dead, even after being shot down in front of your eyes. Now, I have pulled that power out of him and placed it into this," she said, indicating the bag. With her other hand, she took a match from her pocket, struck it against the wooden boardwalk and touched it to the bag. "His power is no more!"

And with that last word, she tossed the bag to the ground near the stairs just as the flames consumed the little pouch. When it hit the mud, not only did the bag explode, but the ground on which it landed burst into a ball of flame as though the earth itself had banished the contents of the bag to hell.

Stokes watched as the piece of ground flared and burned. The mud and weeds popped and crackled, giving off a black smoke. When he saw that bag destroyed, he felt that nagging voice in the back of his head get snuffed out as well. Suddenly, he saw himself as a free man. The faces of his wife and child rushed to the front of his thoughts while Rhyse became nothing more than a bad dream . . . a crazy old man.

Monique hadn't taken her eyes off Stokes from the moment she'd flung her pouch of gunpowder onto the metal plate that Clint had set down earlier. She'd seen the look on his face several times. It was the same look worn by the people who came into her mother's parlor asking for the impossible. That same look had been directed at her when she'd visited homes in other towns and mixed up "love potions" that were nothing more than bitter-tasting wine.

That expression was one of belief. Monique had found that, with a little belief, people could do amazing things for their own lives. Sometimes they just needed a push to get the belief they needed. Some would call it cheating, but to Monique and Cleo it was a simple way to make people feel and live better. But most of all, it worked. It certainly worked for Willie Stokes.

By the time Clint and Joseph had walked up to Stokes, they'd wiped off most of the paste from their faces. When Stokes looked at them, he no longer saw rotting corpses or painted warriors. All he saw was two men with some mud on their faces.

"You're no witch," Stokes said as he let his rifle drop to the ground. "An' now I can see what a fool I was for following a man like Rhyse."

Clint stepped forward and put a hand on Stokes's shoulder. "Rhyse worked awful hard to get you to think like him. And as crazy as he is, he's real good at what he does."

"How can I go back to my old life after what I've seen? Nobody would be fool enough to live in the same town as me."

"That power's gone now," Clint said while pointing down to the fire that still burned at their feet. "It's gone and everybody knows it."

Looking up, Stokes could see that they were not alone on the street. There were faces peeking out from nearly every window and poking around from scattered corners all up and down the road. Already they were whispering and gossiping amongst themselves. Already the word was spreading as to what had happened and anyone with eyes could tell that it wouldn't take long at all for word to spread through the town, spilling out to other towns in every direction.

The side door to one of the nearby buildings squeaked open and an old man in a long nightshirt hobbled outside to look at the group by the burning ground with concern etched across his face. "Are you folks all right?" he asked.

Stokes reached up with both hands and rubbed at the mud on his face. When he smiled, the mask of paste cracked all the way down to his skin. "I feel better now than I have in a long time." He then turned and looked down at Monique. "Thank you."

FORTY-TWO

"I can hear something goin' on out there!" Rhyse ranted from his cell. "It's my congregation come to set me free! You'd best let me go now before you are swept away by the whirlwind."

There were two deputies and Sheriff Brody inside the office. The sheriff was standing at the front door, ready to act in case Clint's plan went out of control. He cursed himself for being talked into letting Clint have free reign, but he was pleasantly surprised when he saw the big black fella throw down his gun and smile.

Standing next to Brody was a young deputy named Tim Vashon. Tim was supposed to help keep an eye on the prisoner, but for the moment he was riveted by the display taking place outside. "I'll be damned," Tim said in a soft, stunned voice. "I never knew Miss Monique had that kind'a fire. She just plucked the devil right out of that man."

Brody shook his head quietly, not buying into the show for one minute. But as he scanned the faces of the people looking on from their windows and doors, he could tell that he was in the minority.

Inside the office, toward the back of the squat building, Deputy Allan Metteaux wanted desperately to see what all the outside fuss was about, but didn't allow himself to leave his prisoner. He squirmed on the little three-legged stool, taking the occasional glance out the room's only barred window.

177

He'd seen Miss Monique do her fair share of good. He'd even been into Byers to meet Madame Cleo, but he'd only heard stories about this kind of thing happening.

From within a corner of the room, sectioned off by two walls of wood and two of steel bars, Mason Rhyse threw himself against the door of his prison like a wild animal at the end of a chain. "I've got to get out there! If you let me go, I may see fit to let you live."

"Shut the hell up, old man," Metteaux barked. He tried to take comfort from the fact that Rhyse was behind bars, but he still couldn't help but be more than a little frightened of him.

The way he raged inside that cell, Rhyse looked possessed. And from the stories going around, possessed was exactly what he was.

Suddenly, as if sensing what was going on inside the deputy's head, Rhyse became absolutely still. His body was unnaturally rigid and his face was pressed up against the bars. "Get over here, boy," he said in a voice that radiated power, even from the inside of a cage.

Metteaux turned his youthful face over to the prisoner and was struck by how sunken the old man's eyes were and how pasty his flesh looked in the flickering light of the room's only lantern. "Just . . . just sit down . . . and shut up, I told ya."

"My voice is failin' me," Rhyse croaked. "I need you to tell the sheriff somethin'. It's about that man outside . . ." Pausing, Rhyse cringed in pain and coughed up in ragged breaths. ". . . that black man . . . he'll kill any . . ."

After all the screaming he'd been doing, Rhyse's voice drifted off and became a haggard whisper. Metteaux heard the part about someone getting killed and leaned in closer to see if he could pick up the rest. As soon as he was within range, Rhyse's hand shot out from between the bars and wrapped around the deputy's throat.

Metteaux tried to call out for help, but his Adam's apple was being crushed inside the preacher's bony fingers. Dark blurs started to cloud his vision, but he could just make out the back of Tim Vashon's head as the other deputy strained to see what was going on outside.

Hissing like a venomous snake, Rhyse reached out to lift Metteaux's pistol from its holster. "Gimme the keys," he whispered as he pressed the barrel of the gun into the young deputy's back. "And be quiet about it or I'll blow your backbone out through yer stomach."

Metteaux did as he was told. He tried to stall long enough for one of the others to notice what was happening, but they all seemed transfixed by whatever it was they were watching. His hand fumbled with the keys and then awkwardly handed them to the madman behind him.

Snatching the keys from Metteaux, Rhyse fitted them into the lock until one of them turned. Prodding Metteaux with the gun, he opened the door and stepped outside before slamming the side of the pistol against the back of the deputy's head. When Metteaux's body crashed to the floor, the sheriff and his deputy spun around, grabbing for their guns.

Rhyse pointed and fired, his eyes barely even focused on anything else besides the door. If he'd been more than ten feet away, he would have missed completely. But since he'd been charging out of that cell as fast as his legs could carry him, he managed to put a bullet through Sheriff Brody's ribs and another into his hip.

The impact of the bullets rocked the lawman back off his feet, but he still managed to pull his gun free just before he hit the floor. Deputy Vashon felt fear grip him like a cold hand wrapped around his heart. He tried to draw, but got his pistol caught on the edge of its holster.

Rhyse glared at him as he ran straight into the boy. His eyes were those of a beast, with not even a hint of humanity behind them. "I'll come back for you," he whispered in a voice that trembled beneath the weight of his insanity. "I'll bring you back as one of my own."

The gun went off, but with the barrel dug deep into the deputy's stomach, the blast was muffled until it exploded out of Vashon's back.

Clint spun around as the sounds of gunfire echoed in the street. They were coming from the sheriff's office and without checking to see who was with him, he took off in that direction.

He made it to the front of the office just in time to see Mason Rhyse come staggering out. The preacher walked like he was drunk, clutching a pistol in a shaky hand that was slick with gore and blackened with gunpowder. Clint took in the scene with a single glance. He saw the sheriff struggling on the ground next to the unmoving body of one of the young deputies.

Rhyse stumbled forward. His head lolled on his shoulders, looking around as if in confusion to take in the world that was crumbling on top of him. He saw Clint, the man who shrugged aside his sermons like they meant nothing. Stokes stood nearby, consorting with the witch. "Come back to me!" he screamed.

"Put the gun down, Rhyse," Clint commanded with one hand out and the other on his holstered pistol. "Don't make me—"

"I'll come back! I'll claw my way through the gates of hell!"

Rhyse's hand jerked, bringing the stolen gun up to bear on Clint simply because he was the closest man he could see.

Letting his reflexes take over, Clint moved like a flicker of lightning. His hand snapped the gun from its holster and fired, all before Rhyse's finger could tense on the trigger. The gun in Clint's hand barked once, spitting lead through the air and then through Rhyse's skull, dropping the preacher flat on his back in the sheriff's doorway.

Those watching the scene held their breath, half expecting Rhyse to get up as he did in front of the Zeller estate. But the old man's only movements were the twitching of his leg as his life drained out of him through the fresh hole in his head.

"No more ghost stories," Clint whispered over Rhyse's body. "Not from you."

FORTY-THREE

Clint stayed in Jespin for another few days, mainly to help the sheriff until he recovered from his wounds. Brody had been shot up pretty bad, but the lawman was tough enough to grit his teeth and bear the pain. Luckily, both of Rhyse's shots had gone completely through and hadn't torn apart anything too important.

Even though thoughts of his family weighed heavily on his mind, Stokes walked himself into one of the town's jail cells to await a trial for what he'd done during his time with Mason Rhyse. There were only two cells in the sheriff's office and the instant he'd stepped into one of them, Stokes's eyes went wide and he began to nervously fidget until he could move to the other cell.

The one he'd left was the one where Rhyse had spent some of the last moments of his life. How Stokes knew that was anybody's guess.

It was just after noon on his second day as acting deputy when Clint was pulled aside by Allan Metteaux. The younger deputy shook Clint's hand while looking at him with a mixture of gratitude and admiration. "I jus' want to thank you again Mister Adams, for what you did. If you hadn't stepped in, I'm sure that crazy man would've killed me and Sheriff Brody next."

"For the last time, you're welcome," Clint said.

"Old Miss Wilson down at the general store said that the

town's decided to let Carl Ambrose take over as sheriff until Brody gets back on his feet."

"That's great news," Clint replied, trying not to sound too anxious to get out of town. "Things seem to be pretty quiet around here, so I guess it's all right for me to head out."

Metteaux still hadn't let go of Clint's hand and was shaking it vigorously. "She also told me about you. You're the Gunsmith. You're a famous man."

"I think famous is a bit strong, but . . ."

"If I don't see you before you leave, I want you to know that I'm fixin' to open up a restaurant here in town since I don't seem to be cut out for a deputy. You'll have a big supper waitin' for you any time you come back after it's built."

Clint nodded and walked to the cells in the rear of the office. The door to the back room was open and Clint could just make out the back of Stokes's head. Even lying down, the big man took up most of the space in the cramped quarters. His body hung over the edges of the cot and his knuckles brushed the floor.

"OK, Stokes," Clint said. "I'm going to be leaving now. You're not going to try a jail break after I'm gone are you?"

Without turning around, Stokes started to laugh. His broad shoulders shook up and down and his deep voice bounced off the walls. "Nah. Even since Miss Monique opened my eyes, I've been too damn tired to do much of anythin'."

"Well, you should be able to rest fairly easy. I've been talking to her and the sheriff and it seems like Rhyse did all the crimes they'd hang somebody for. You'll be in here for a while, but you'll see your family again. If you'd like, I can have somebody send for them to see you even sooner. Byers isn't that far away."

"Thanks, but no. When I see 'em it won't be from a cage."

"Suit yourself, but just let one of the deputies know and they can get word out to Byers if you change your mind."

Now, Stokes swung his feet down from the cot and stood up against the bars. "About everythin' I put you through . . . me an' the others . . . I just don't have the words."

"Forget about it," Clint said. "Forget about Rhyse and all the rest of it. Just serve your time and live your life. After that, things will be set right eventually."

Clint left the sheriff's office and headed back to the saloon.

Monique was waiting for him upstairs. Their room smelled like both of them and the sweaty nights they'd spent in Jespin. At the moment, she was sitting in front of the open window. A breeze blew across her skin and made the beads in her hair rattle like gentle rain on a metal roof.

"They've found someone to take over for me," Clint said as he slid up behind her. "Looks like it's time for us to head back."

Monique turned and put her head on Clint's shoulder. "I'm sure Mother is about to lose her mind with worry. But I still wish we could stay awhile longer."

"I'll ride with you back to Byers. After that . . ."

Her face clouded over a bit and she squeezed him tighter. "Would you stay longer if I threatened to curse you?"

Clint shuddered dramatically. "A few days ago, I might have laughed at that. Now, I'm starting to wonder if I should be worried about getting you upset. After all," he said as he held her out at arm's length, "you're the witch of the swamps."

Pulling away from him, Monique slapped Clint lightly on the shoulder. "I'm no witch. That's my mother you're thinking about."

"I'll be sure to tell her that when we get back."

They took their time getting ready to leave. Just when he was about to walk out the door, Monique slipped her dress off her shoulders and pulled him back to the bed where they made slow, passionate love to each other.

By the time they left, the sun was beginning to dip below the horizon. Fortunately, Clint had become all too familiar with the bayou at night.

FORTY-FOUR

Madame Cleo came rushing out to greet Clint and her daughter in a flurry of brightly colored robes and a wave of scrambling felines. She wrapped her arms around Monique and lifted her off the ground as though she was still an infant.

"Oh, my darlin' girl, I was so worried I'd lost you," Cleo gushed. "I've heard that you were busy in Jespin an' I want you to tell me all about it."

Ushering Monique into the house, Cleo waved for Clint to follow her. He stepped inside, thinking that it felt like years since he'd been in the book-lined parlor and the halls that smelled like lemon pie. He looked at the window as he stepped in and, sure enough, there was a freshly baked dessert cooling on the sill.

"I've got something for you," Clint said once they were all inside. He reached into his pocket and removed the dented copper flask. "Rhyse used this mixture to knock people out and I'll tell you firsthand that it worked."

Madame Cleo took the flask, opened it and sniffed the contents. Almost immediately, she pulled her face away, looking as though she'd smelled sour milk. "Oh, that's strong stuff," she said while twisting the cap tightly back in place.

"I figured you could get some use out of it. Maybe for medicine or something. I'm just glad to get it out of my sight."

"Hmmm, it could be a painkiller, 'dats for sure." Setting the flask on a high shelf in her parlor, she added, "Or I could use it on some of these randy young men comin' in 'ere want-in' me to make every girl in the county lust after them."

Monique stood in the hallway, her arms folded across her chest. "It's a curare mixture, Mother. We should probably just dump it outside."

Waving her daughter aside as she scooted down the hall, Cleo busied herself in the kitchen. "We ain't throwin' nothin' outside, child. When you gonna learn not to waste?"

Clint let the squat little woman go about her tasks. Monique stayed behind with him and nestled herself in his arms.

"You're leavin' now, I guess?" she asked.

"It's time, Monique. I was on my way to Texas and there's probably plenty of people wondering where I am as it is. Besides, I think I've had my fill of life in the swamps."

"You'll miss it."

Leaning down, Clint gave Monique a kiss that brought back the desire he'd felt every night since they'd met. Her lips were full and soft. He savored his last sample of the taste of her, which was somehow sweet and spicy at the same time. "I won't miss it as much as I'll miss you," he said. "Tell Cleo I said good-bye. I have a feeling if I tell her myself, she'll rope me into staying for more of her pie and I don't want to ruin my appetite."

Once he was sitting in the small cabin once again occupied by Joseph and Kim Terray, Clint felt all the strangeness from the last several days drift away. The shapely redhead maneuvered around the stove, stirring pots of various sizes and checking on a tray of cornbread muffins browning in the heat. The smell was enough to make Clint's mouth water.

Joseph stood looking out the window. He hadn't wanted to stay around Jespin any longer than he had to and, thanks to Clint's assurances that Joseph was a kidnapped victim and not a robber, Sheriff Brody had let him go.

He'd been home for a few days now. Standing at a window, Joseph stared out at the bayou and took a deep breath. "I thought I'd never taste Kim's cookin' again." Turning to Clint, he added, "And I got you to thank for bein' here."

"You want to thank me? Then let me have extra helpings of that gumbo I smell."

Kim moved up behind her husband and wrapped her arms

around his chest. "This is all like a dream come true. Last I knew, my husband was dead an' he wasn't coming back. Now . . . everything's perfect."

"Not quite everything," Clint said as he sat down at the table which was all set for the night's meal.

He wasn't able to make himself wait for Kim and Joseph to sit down before he tore off a piece of cornbread and ladled a generous helping of gumbo into his bowl. The concoction was spicy enough to singe his nostrils when he leaned over the bowl.

Just the way he liked it.

Almost like a ritual, Clint slowly pulled his bread in half, dipped it into the gumbo and took a bite.

He thought about all the running he'd done through those damn swamps and all the twisted paths he'd had to cross just to get to this moment. And when that bread melted in his mouth, leaving nothing but a smoothly textured layer of sweet corn soaked with all those rich spices and bits of tender meat, he realized one thing.

It was all worth it.

Watch for

THE CHEROKEE STRIP

236th novel in the exciting GUNSMITH series
from Jove

Coming in August!